Vertical Hold
Soulful Tales of Our Keeping God

Short Stories by Deborah J. Glover

To Ms Anita
Many thanks
Deborah
6/2017

Vertical Hold

*"The LORD makes firm the steps
of the one who delights in him;
though he may stumble, he will not fall, for the LORD
upholds him with his hand."
~Psalm 37:23-24 NIV*

Also By The Author

Songs from the Cross: Poetic Expressions from a Disciple of Christ

Acknowledgements

I'd like to extend my sincere appreciation to Nakia Phelps, my graphic designer. You understood my vision and adorned *Vertical Hold* in beauty and grace. I'm also grateful to a host of gifted editorial contributors who labored with me on this project. Thank you, Nadiyah M. Jett, Kamille D. Whittaker, and Anita L. Clay. Sometimes it takes a village! It was a blessing to have your talents at work on my first book of short stories.

Most of all, I am increasingly grateful to God as He keeps me on the wheel. I thank You, Lord Jesus, for manifold tools of discipleship and for every word that I've been graced to pen. Glory to Your name!

DJG

Dedication

To all the seers that love and pray.

TABLE OF CONTENTS

Crossroads[7]

Sifting the Squeeze[30]

Not by Works[63]

Offerings[88]

Gongs and Cymbals[101]

Suggested Reading Group
Questions[114]

Crossroads

"Love and faithfulness meet together;
righteousness and peace kiss each other."
~Psalm 85:10

Crossroads

In 1962, Greenwich Village was a magnet for performers, artists, and free thinkers from different backgrounds. Color blindness set the tone for varied expressions of cultural diversity. Many improbable ties were formed — some by way of divine intervention.

Social activism found its voice in local stage plays. Early that year, the news broke about an urban-centric remake of *The Defiant Ones*. The lead roles, portrayed so brilliantly on screen by Sidney Poitier and Tony Curtis would be brought to the stage by Isaac Walker and Luke Prince.

Isaac's contribution to the theater project was threefold. In addition to sharing the lead with Luke, he had also written and directed the stage adaptation.

As opening night approached, some critics had doubts regarding the transition of this racially charged drama to live theater. However, by the time the Village Door Playhouse wrapped up its glorious 24-week run, former skeptics were singing praises from Broadway to Hollywood. The play turned out to be an unprecedented hit for New York's Freedom Arts Theater Troupe.

Born and raised in Brooklyn, Isaac still called Bedford-Stuyvesant home when he was not on the road. Needless to say, this tour had been a timely blessing, granting him the priceless fellowship of family and friends.

Unfortunately, the Big Apple offered a different comfort to Luke. The native Mississippian had a reputation for women and alcohol. Whenever the curtain came down, Luke hardened his heart to the still, small voice and said *yes*, to the lusts of the flesh. No one seemed to care – as long as he delivered on stage.

Isaac had witnessed the destruction of many gifted actors who'd fallen in pursuit of the Great White Way. If not for the grace that much more abounds, he too would have answered that siren call. However, in his time of need, God kept him. And so, led by something beyond his control, Isaac decided to intervene in the life of his co-star.

Riding the high of their final performance, the cast members changed and went separate ways. The finale was a matinee swan song to make everyone proud.

Isaac left the theater with his mind set on a sure to please home cooked meal. As he was heading down West 4th Street to the subway station, Luke was easing himself onto the chair of a sidewalk café up ahead, ordering a Heineken.

"Hey, man, mind if I join you?"

It was surely not Isaac's idea to pull up a seat and ask for a menu. But there he was. And although he'd never admit such a thing, his lonely, soon-to-be-friend was very grateful.

Luke watched Isaac peruse the menu, hoping he'd find something. He didn't want to eat alone.

"So how's the food here?"

"It's not bad. A native New Yorker like yourself should find something appealing."

"Well, Luke, I don't know about that. There are eight million people in the Naked City and almost as many types of cuisine. In any case, the best food in town comes out of Brooklyn."

"Is that so, where about?"

"My family's house, as a matter of fact, they're getting ready to chow down as we speak!"

Luke heard himself ask, "Is that an invitation?"

Isaac replied, "Let's go."

Luke paid his tab and the two hurried toward the train station. An admiring waitress smiled after them, pocketing her tip as she cleared away Luke's untouched beer.

It was simply too hot for May. Every window was open and the electric fans were at full speed. The aroma from 261 Halsey Street permeated the air and each passerby couldn't help but wish that they had an invitation to dinner. Dana finished icing the chocolate cake and checked the clock.

"Kitty, please baste the roast once more and turn off the collards."

"Okay Sis, I think these sweet potato pies can come out as well. The macaroni and cheese just has to brown and then we can turn this oven off. Girl, you put your foot in this fried chicken!"

9

"Hey, Momma Walker's recipe never fails. I sure hope nothing's gone wrong on the subway. Isaac should have been home by now."

"Dana, you know that nothing stops the A Train. I'll bet some star-struck fan has unwittingly given my husband an opening to testify. And you can believe she walked away with more than she bargained for. Poor Isaac, so fine and not a clue!"

Dana laughed with her sister-in-law, loving her sense of security. Unsolicited female attention was an occupational hazard for the handsome actor and many women were undeterred by his marital status. But Kitty never responded with jealousy and mistrust. As a couple, they vowed to give the adversary no room to operate.

All of a sudden, the sound of Dee Dee Sharp's "Mashed Potato Time" broke forth from the record player. The family was getting restless.

"Dana, I think they're trying to tell us something."

Dana winked at Kitty and proclaimed in a loud voice, "Well, I don't know how much longer we can hold back that starving multitude upfront."

A voice from the living room responded to Dana. "I know that's right!"

Someone else called out, "Yeah, Dana, the smells from those pots are about to start a riot up in here!"

"Okay, family, just give him a few minutes more. We don't always have Isaac in town. Let's show him some love."

Cousin Melvin was quick to reply, "Dana, he's been here six months. We can love him and eat at the same time."

Dana and Kitty looked at each other, shaking their heads in feigned disgust.

The two women met during their freshman year at Hunter College. Kitty, a native of Louisiana, needed a suitable watch care ministry, during her sojourn from the Big Easy. Dana invited her to church and that's where she met Isaac.

It was a mutual case of love at first sight. But, neither of them would have their individual goals derailed by a premature marriage.

Kitty's path became clear when Rosa Parks refused to give up her seat on the bus. Gazing at that photo of Rosa being fingerprinted, she saw the embodiment of every person who'd crossed paths with injustice and refused to back down. Because of that woman's quiet courage, Kitty decided to become a civil rights attorney.

She was passionate about her calling and shared her intentions with Isaac the day they met. He was blown away by this fiery young woman, who knew who she was and where she was going. In the course of time, Isaac would encourage his lovely soul mate all the way through law school. The two were married soon after she passed her bar exam.

Much like Kitty, Isaac had his own calling. He fell in love with the theater as a fifth grader. When P.S. 44 did its rendition of *The King and I*, he had the lead role. From that point on, if the boy was not acting in a school play he most surely had a hand in its production.

None of Isaac's fellow grads from N.Y.U.'s class of '53 were surprised when the stage became his vehicle for civil action. Throughout his career, he would use the theater to promote social consciousness and rally for change.

Kitty believed in her husband's work and understood its importance. Although she and Isaac had different talents, they found ways to use them in tandem. They shared the same dream.

It was an exciting time to be alive. The push for civil rights ushered in a reawakening and celebration of black culture not seen since the Harlem Renaissance.

But, by the time Kitty and Isaac turned to afros and dashikis as a means of ethnic expression, Jesus had already confirmed their worth in the Father. They knew black was beautiful before it became a catchphrase. And they lived it without diminishing any other segment of humanity.

When other doctrines began to denounce Christianity as a racist white man's religion, the couple was not deceived. They acknowledged Jesus as the true Great Emancipator. Because of their faith, Isaac and Kitty were seen as role models by many of their fellow believers.

As the train pulled into Kingston and Throop Station, Isaac slapped his companion on the shoulder. "This is it man, my home turf!"

They took the subway stairs three at a time, coming out on Fulton Street. Immediately, Luke was consumed by the sights and sounds of Bed-Stuy. Soulful rhythms filled the air – echoes of another time and place. He marveled inwardly, *I can't believe I'm here!*

Lost in thought, Luke barely heard Isaac's impromptu lesson on black urban culture.

"There's the Brooklyn Apollo and Club Baby Grand is just a few blocks over. Our church, Berean House, is coming up on the left. My dad was a minister like his father before him. I guess I chose a slightly different pulpit. My parents migrated from down South in the 1920s. They were among the first people of color to purchase a home when the neighborhood changed over…"

And so Isaac continued the history lesson, virtually wasted on his companion.

Meanwhile, the two of them were totally oblivious to the stares from people on the street. Both Isaac and Luke stood over six feet tall and every inch was spectacular to behold.

Isaac was mocha chocolate, with large deep-set eyes trimmed in thick lashes. His dimpled smile revealed a brilliant flash of white made more appealing by the tiny gap between his two front teeth. A Caesar haircut perfectly complemented his neatly trimmed goatee.

Luke's blond silky waves had been streaked by the sun. His face was clean shaven except for prominent brows that threatened to meet above his perfectly chiseled nose. High cheekbones complimented a strong jaw line that ended rather squarely at the chin. His eyes changed color like the sea – sometimes blue, sometimes green, but always disarming.

This gorgeous duo from opposite ends of the color spectrum strode together almost as one, hurrying toward their destination. The play of contrast and similarity managed to startle and embrace the senses all at once. One couldn't blame the onlookers. They would have drawn attention in any neighborhood!

Halsey Street was not far from the train station, so they reached Isaac's block in no time. Just a few paces from the corner stood the well-kept brownstone. This was the place Isaac's family had called home for over two decades. The laughter of loved ones and the smell of good food called to them as they entered the yard. One entered with the assurance of belonging; the other desperately longed to belong.

"Melvin, was that the gate?"

Melvin glanced out of the window and replied back to Dana. "Ah, yeah Dana, they're here."

Before Dana could say, "*They* who?" the doorway was filled with Isaac…and with Luke.

Now Isaac loved the way Kitty welcomed him home, whether their separation had been days or hours. "Hi baby, how'd it go?"

"It went just fine, my love."

Luke and Dana nodded hello. Then, while glancing over at Kitty and Isaac, they playfully cleared their throats almost in sync. This caused the love birds to loosen their embrace and turn to Luke who was grinning nervously at no one in particular.

"Sorry man, I've forgotten my manners. Actually, I believe you all met opening night, but Luke, this is my wife, Kitty, and my sister, Dana."

Dana replied, "Yes indeed, I remember opening night. Welcome, Luke. I hope you brought your appetite!"

Kitty jumped in with, "Hello, Luke. Honey, introduce him to everybody while we dish up the food."

The two men walked into the living room, where Isaac announced, "Everybody listen up. This is Luke."

A jovial chorus of, "Hi Luke!" filled the room.

Then, with a mischievous grin, Isaac continued, "And relax, he's white, but he doesn't seem to know it." They all laughed as Luke blushed right through his tan.

That first dinner with Isaac and his family turned out to be a life changing experience for Luke. Over the following months, he became a regular at their home and was soon welcomed into their church fellowship.

Pastor Isaac Walker Sr. had gone home to Jesus the year before. His young mentee, Hosea Nixon, had been the undisputed choice to succeed him as pastor of the Berean House fellowship. It turned out to be a wise decision for the growing congregation.

One Sunday Pastor Nixon preached a message entitled, "God's Unchanging Love." It was a healing word to Luke's parched soul. When the message ended, he went forward and fell on the altar, grateful and unashamed.

As Isaac knelt down beside his friend, Berean House was struck color-blind. Every heart rejoiced for another wayward son who'd returned to the Father.

From then on, Luke and his three new siblings-in-Christ spent a lot of time together. Luke desired the contentment that Isaac exuded, evidence of his submission to Jesus. Isaac became the much needed mentor and friend for the man who had yet to expose himself, fully. The Lord would orchestrate that next crossroad at His appointed time.

Luke's performance during the Greenwich Village stage production resulted in a number of promising offers that he'd have to assess through a new set of values. Meanwhile, he was doing some modeling and commercial work.

Unfortunately, Isaac's equally brilliant performance did not generate the same opportunities. But he was undeterred, focusing on writing a new play for his theater ensemble and teaching drama at a neighborhood center.

Kitty had begun looking into avenues where she might be of

assistance with the desegregation efforts in the South, while Dana remained devoted to her elementary school students.

Dana was a gifted teacher and a blessing to the children in her class. She believed in each of them, and poured herself out until they believed in themselves.

That year, when school closed for the summer, Dana convinced Berean House to open a vacation Bible camp. Every kid able to scrape up 50 cents a week was eligible to participate in the creative Bible activities, field trips, and tasty home cooked lunches offered throughout the summer. Despite the registration fee set by the church board, Dana turned no child away.

A certain little boy from public school was one of her favorites. He lagged behind the other kids during registration that first morning, painfully aware of his empty pockets. But Dana was delighted to see him.

"Seth, come on in here, precious. It's okay, sweetheart, you just draw me something pretty."

Luke worked with Dana in the youth ministry. He shared her desire to reach the children who had seen more of life's sorrow than its joy. Together, they labored to bring them to a genuine understanding of Jesus and their value in the Father. As a result of their efforts, several of those precious ones returned to public school having found their voice.

Dana was fast becoming Luke's *shero,* as she shared her vision and hope with him for these young people, all but forgotten by mainstream America.

It was easy to see that Isaac and Dana were siblings. Luke was deeply moved as he beheld their resemblance. And he beheld Dana every chance he got!

She had Isaac's same flawless coloring. Her long lashes framed an arresting gaze that drew you in and held you captive. Then, as if to soften the impact, her lips parted to reveal the signature dimpled smile.

Those comely features were passed down from their mother, the late Mrs. Mildred Walker. Standing almost six feet tall, Dana inherited her stature from Isaac Walker Sr.

Although women's fashion was greatly influenced by the nation's First Lady, Dana created her own style as she mixed Camelot with a little bit of soul. Each classic silhouette was tastefully chosen to compliment her well-toned curves, without a breach of modesty.

Yes indeed, from Luke's point of view, Dana was a fine woman from the inside-out.

In New York, you made the most of Indian summer. Luke came over one Saturday morning to join Isaac for a game of handball in Tompkins Park. As Dana watched them turn the corner on their bikes, her sister-in-law walked up the steps and sat beside her on the stoop. Kitty's seersucker culottes offered little protection from the hot surface. Dana's cotton pedal pushers were not much better.

"I think we could use some padding," Kitty said, grabbing two pillows from the vestibule. For a moment they sat in silence watching a little girl jump double Dutch until her friends thought their arms would fall off.

Kitty's auburn curls were ablaze in the morning sun. Freckles were in full bloom across her pale cheeks. She turned to Dana, who smiled weakly, looking away from the amber brown eyes that saw the truth. Kitty hurt for her, and for what she was about to do. But, she had heard clearly and would obey.

"So, what are you two going to do? "

"What do you mean?" Dana replied, knowing exactly what her sister-friend meant.

Kitty breathed a silent prayer. *Okay Lord, please help me here.*

"Well, Sis, you and Luke are in love. What are you going to do?"

Dana shook her head, trying not to tear up.

"I don't know. He has this notion that we should marry, but I don't know, Kitty. His color won't open any doors for us, but my color will surely cause doors to close in our faces.

Married to me, he'll suddenly find himself constrained, unable to come and go as he pleases. So many of the freedoms he's taken for granted will be lost. I couldn't bear to see resentment or regret in his eyes."

Kitty looked at her in disbelief.

"Dana, it's pretty obvious from his conversation that Luke is not blind to the racist attitudes of his people. Evidently, he's already counted the cost. But Dana, have you taken into consideration what you'd stand to lose?"

"What do you mean?"

"Well, have you considered the demeaning legacy of interaction between white men and black women? Marriage to a white man could very well cause some colored doors to close in your faces. Our church is not the whole world you know…no pun intended."

Dana tried to smile but her eyes were filling up. She reached in her pocket for a tissue as Kitty pressed on.

"If confronted with the alienation of your people, could you one day look at Luke with regret in your eyes – say if he failed to relate to your struggle?"

"No, Kitty, that's not Luke. His ability to relate is one of the many things I love about him. He's passionate about civil rights and racial equality."

Kitty smiled, nodding her agreement.

"Yes, he's made that quite clear as well. Dana, is it not then reasonable to conclude that your fears should not determine your course of action? Listen, after you've counted the cost this is really about the two of you. Case closed."

But Dana was not relieved by Kitty's summation. She hadn't considered the rejection of her own people. Now, a frustrated mix of emotions rose to the surface.

"Okay, Kitty, you make a logical argument. But I don't need a lawyer's assessment right now. Hearts are lost under the most illogical circumstances. Can you cut the logic? I'm in trouble and I need some straight-talk!"

Kitty's tone was equally confrontational as she replied, "Okay, Sis, I'll oblige you."

The day had warmed up to be another Brooklyn scorcher. It was time to go inside. Kitty stood up and started back down the steps. Then Dana followed, slightly puzzled by her sister-in-law's response. But she was about to get the straight-talk she'd asked for.

Seated at the kitchen table with a pitcher of lemonade, the two women resumed their conversation.

"Dana, did you ever wonder why my family has never visited, or why my own parents did not attend my wedding?"

Before Dana could reply, Kitty lit into her in a way that made Dana rear back in her chair.

"Of course you did, but you were too polite to press the issue when I offered up my lame excuses. Then I swore my husband to secrecy, which he has honored all this time.

Well, now, I'm going to open up the closet and let the skeletons fall out where they may. Perhaps it will keep you from making the same mistake my mother made before she ever had me."

Kitty pulled her tousled hair into a rubber band as if preparing to throw down. She then began her story.

"Dana, there has been a color line among the non-white folk in Louisiana since the time of slavery. In 1930, my mother was a lovely fair-skinned debutante preparing to take her place in society.

Then, she met and fell in love with a very dark-skinned man from the other side of the tracks. When she became pregnant, my grandparents' response was to put her under virtual house arrest until the child was born.

Her precious brown-skinned baby was delivered at home and immediately given over to some poor excuse for an orphanage, where he died before his first birthday.

Meanwhile, my grandparents had to find a suitable (high yellow) man still willing to marry her. You see, she had brought public shame to the family because of her lowly association.

In the end, Momma gave in to an asinine social order that crushed her spirit and coerced her into marrying the man who would become my father. I saw what a loveless but "acceptable" union was like, up close and personal.

Dana, life and love are too precious to surrender up to the dictates of bigotry. That's why when I fell in love with your brother nothing was going to keep my Howdy Doody-looking behind from marrying him.

Yes, I did count the cost. It cost me my family but I have never regretted that decision. Because I knew it was really about the two of us, and the One who would join us together."

Kitty reached across the table to grasp Dana's hands and smiled at the contrast.

"And finally my beloved, we know that the Christian warning against mixed marriage has nothing to do with skin color. There is a Biblical warning to the saved regarding their fellowship with the unsaved. But that's all about *spiritual* darkness mixing with *spiritual* light.

Although Luke was back-sliding when you first met him, his salvation was not in question. And no one can deny the way his life has turned around before our very eyes. So I repeat Sister-love, what are you two going to do?"

Dana would spend the next few months in the valley of decision.

The warmth of autumn had continued after its passing. It was a mild winter evening. Luke had returned from a delicious fish fry at the Walkers' and was home alone in private self-reflection.

God had granted him a glimpse of what was possible. Dana's love was possible. Adoration fell short of describing Luke's feelings for her. She was everything he considered fine and good, everything his life had denied him for so many years. In her company, Luke was beside himself with joy and to his astonishment she returned his affection.

Dana evoked feelings almost too intense to contain. But, she was not another score to be added to his list of wanton conquests.

Apart from Isaac and Kitty, Luke had one other frame of reference for this love and the righteous intentions it inspired.

He rose from the studio couch and sat down at his desk, which doubled as a dining table. From the drawer, he pulled out a well-worn Bible. Inside were his two most precious possessions. One was a group photo of the Prince family standing with a minister in front of a large tent. The other was an individual portrait of his mother.

Leaning them up against the Bible, he recalled the day they were taken. Fighting back tears, wanting desperately to will his very being back through time and space, he whispered, *"Lord, I'm so tired of running, so tired of hiding."*

Just then, the doorbell rang. Luke checked his watch. It was 11:00 pm. He considered ignoring it, having lost his appetite for the kind of company that showed up late and uninvited. But something led him to the door.

"Who is it?"

"Luke, it's me, Dana."

He opened the door and she stepped in bringing light into his tiny space.

"Hi, Dana how'd you get here? I mean, please have a seat. Let me take your jacket. Would you like a Pepsi?"

His discomfort made her want to run into his arms.

Okay girl. That would not glorify God.

So, she sat down on the couch instead, and answered his questions.

"Actually I borrowed my cousin's Impala, and, yes I'd love a Pepsi, thanks."

"Great, I'll be right back."

As Luke searched the kitchen for two clean glasses and emptied the ice tray into a bowl, Dana walked around his shabby, not-so-chic apartment.

"Oh, no…" Luke exhaled as he rushed back into the living room. But it was too late. Dana was staring at the photos.

"Luke, I'm confused…that minister is my father!"

"I know, Dana. I recognized him from the photos in your home."

Dana dropped into the chair not believing her eyes and ears. She turned away from Luke's pained expression to stare once again at the pictures.

"Now I know this is you in the photo. But, who are these other people with you? Who is this beautiful woman?"

Luke sat down on the couch and held out his hand to the woman he loved. She came over and sat beside him.

"Dana, I have a lot to confess if you have time."

"Oh, I have time, Luke. Surely I was drawn here tonight for a reason."

Provision intercepted a righteous need, and the lie that had shaped Luke's existence for well over a decade was about to meet its end.

❋❋❋❋❋❋

Mamie Rush was a beautiful colored woman who'd just turned 18 when she met and married Nate Prince. Mamie was the first in her family able to read and write, going as far as the 7th grade.

Nate was the consummate image of tall, dark, and handsome. Every girl around had hopes that he'd pursue her until she caught him. But, he only had eyes for Mamie.

One day, after church, he convinced her to teach him how to read. It was his way of *keeping time* on the sly. However, Nate continued with the lessons even after Mamie accepted his marriage proposal. He was proud of his lady and wanted her to be proud of him. By the time they stood up before the preacher, Mamie's betrothed was able to read and sign his name.

Like all their ancestors since the emancipation, Nate and Mamie were sharecroppers locked in a never ending struggle to survive. Still under the yoke of Jim Crow, neither could imagine anything better for themselves.

But, they loved one another and adored the fruit of that love. The couple dreamed of a better life for their babies and hoped that with an education they might have it. And so, Mr. and Mrs. Prince made a pledge to see their children through school.

During the first few years of marriage, Mamie and Nate were blessed with their two daughters. Coleen and Ruth had their mother's honey maple coloring and long, thick hair. Their daddy gave them his cleft chin and dark, almond shaped eyes. Nate cherished his girls and prayed each day for a son.

Then, Luke was born – ivory skinned with golden hair and blue eyes.

He began his descent into this world as Mamie picked cotton, coming forth before she made it back to the cabin. When her pains started, Nate ran to get Aunt Josie, the beloved matriarch who presided over all the colored births. Mamie's tormented delivery under the relentless Mississippi sun would mark the final issue from her womb.

As the midwife cut the cord and placed Luke at his mother's breast, Mamie beheld her son with resignation. One did not have to look very far to see the resemblance... just across the fields to the landowner's house.

Nate was immediately pulled away from his wife's open air delivery room and surrounded on all sides by the brethren who sharecropped beside him. Each man gathered there was on intimate terms with the anguish of racial oppression. But the immediate, collective job of the group was to keep Nate from any attempt at avenging his wife's rape.

Years of pent up rage found its voice as Nate cried out from the depth of his soul. "I'll kill him. Don't matter what happen to me, long as I kill him! Why can't they leave us be?" He collapsed into the arms of Cal, his closest friend.

"Think Nate, think! So you kill him or try to, then what for Mamie and the young'uns? All you did was to give some crackers the pleasure of lynching you."

Cal's words were no exaggeration. Mississippi soil was drenched with the strange fruit offerings of black men. And the blood was crying out.

The abuse suffered by generations of her maternal lineage had been visited upon Mamie. Like his forefathers before him, Conrad Wooten had occasion to crave the dark and lovely flesh of those he considered inferior but highly serviceable.

When the occasion hit him, he selected married women or virgins – what better way to demonstrate his dominion over the black man? After all, he was entitled and his entitlement transcended any claim to liberty on the part of his inferiors.

So, Mamie bent her back in Conrad's cotton fields and spread her legs at his command. Being summoned to the Wooten home for light chores would more than likely involve this particular burden. She prayed not to conceive, hoping that he'd soon tire of her. And she told no one!

To tell was to put your husband at serious risk. Many colored men who took a stand against the tyranny of Jim Crow were either killed or they simply disappeared to places unknown. Since the end of Reconstruction, thousands had been hauled off to forced labor camps on bogus charges. More than a few died in captivity.

And for years, Washington D.C. had turned a deaf ear to the pleas for help from women who'd lost husbands, sons, and brothers.

Now having suffered Conrad's abuse, Mamie could be sure of

his only self-imposed restriction. Upon planting his seed with proof of life, he was then finished with her. By the time baby Luke took his first breath in the stifling heat, Conrad was inclined to return to his lily white marriage bed where he'd be monogamous for a good while.

And when the occasion hit him again, he'd be sure to seek out new flesh.

All of the landowners in his circle were racist to the core, but few were complicit in his form of oppression. They reasoned that provoking the darkies this way would eventually lead to some form of unrest. And the inevitable backlash that would follow from poor whites eager to do Conrad's dirty work was simply bad for business.

However, Conrad Wooten was either your formidable ally or your very dangerous enemy. So they looked the other way, laughed at his jokes and coveted his dinner invitations. On those occasions, after the ladies were dismissed, Conrad liked to boast of his exploits.

As the colored help served brandy, he'd stoke the flames of their suppressed anger with comments like, "They should have stuck with jumping the broom. At least our ancestors gave them no false expectation of sanctity!"

What then became of Nate and Mamie Prince is another untold American tragedy. Conrad Wooten's violation was an atrocious assault on the love they shared and the vows they had taken, from which they'd find no recompense. Yet, they had to go on like countless others before them. Determined to prevail for their children's sake, the two sought refuge in denial.

Each made an unspoken vow never to discuss what had happened. But that deliberate numbing of anger and pain had its collateral damage. The defilement loomed over and between them each time they reached for one another. And after a time, rote replaced passion on their marriage bed.

Still, the enemy was never satiated. Nate and Mamie watched their girls grow lovelier every day and were very afraid.

Poor Luke was a constant reminder of the thing Nate and Mamie tried to forget. At an early age, the child began to sense that something was wrong, and that he was the cause of it. It wasn't long before he wondered at the obvious difference in his appearance. But some primal fear of knowing outweighed his curiosity. And so, he never asked.

Instead, Luke set out to try and secure his family's affection by becoming Mamie and Nate's most obedient and hardworking child. He would make himself as easy to love as possible. When the truth became apparent to him (albeit unspoken), he was more determined to please than ever.

The fact is that Luke was loved, but the love was always tainted with sorrow. Longing for the easy show of paternal affection demonstrated to his siblings, Luke pretended not to notice Nate's thinly veiled hesitation when he reached out to hug him. He endured the conflicted gaze of his father even as he said to him, "Good job, son."

Meanwhile, Mamie embraced the opposite extreme, as Nate and the girls struggled not to misunderstand. It wasn't that she valued Luke more because of his whiteness. No, she mourned his whiteness. It symbolized the injustice she'd suffered, and it secured his place as a second class member of his own family.

But, because Mamie also saw the boy as her closest co-victim, it drew her to him in a way that the others could never quite grasp.

Having lost the battle for her marriage, she would not lose her son as well. So, she showered him with affection as a buffer from the lukewarm acceptance of his father and sisters.

Even so, Luke could not escape the pitying expressions from Ruth and Coleen when they caught him staring in the mirror. He wanted desperately to look like the people he loved. In time, Luke began to despise that which had denied him that right. There was a quiet, steady, rage taking hold on the inside. But divine intervention was about to unfold.

It was the summer of '46. According to popular religious doctrine, Luke had already passed the age of accountability for sin. He was the only member of the Prince household who still needed to take his place on the mourner's bench and "Get religion."

Ignoring the pleas of their pastor, Nate and Mamie had kept their son from the mourner's bench as long as they could. Luke's paternity was obvious and everyone knew where the guilt belonged. Still, his parents dreaded anything that would expose him to further scrutiny.

However, no one resists the call of one whose time has come. That year, Pastor Rawls broke with tradition, inviting a minister from up North to lead their annual tent meeting. His coming caused quite a fuss among the little congregation.

Some were excited to see and hear the man from New York City. Others were skeptical. But, on the opening day of revival, there was standing room only in the tent. And the mourner's bench was full.

Pastor Isaac Walker Sr. opened their revival with a Biblically sound message of the Gospel. When the sermon ended, Luke confessed Jesus as his Lord and Savior. Up front and center, he was saved and filled with the Spirit. And everyone had an ear to hear what was said to the church as Luke began to proclaim the wonders of God.

Then, Pastor Walker laid hands on the boy and spoke as the Spirit gave utterance.

"What the enemy meant for harm, God is turning for good. Men will see you lifted in humility as another is brought low in pride. After the sifting and the fire, you shall come forth as pure gold to do good works. Beloved son, you are washed by the blood of the Lamb. In the name of Jesus! Amen."

At the time, Luke was just four months away from his 17th birthday. Coleen and Ruth were 18 and 19, respectively.

After graduation, the Prince girls began day work for a white family in town. They still helped in the field during seed time and harvest.

One day, Luke overheard Coleen trying to comfort Ruth on the back porch. Ruth was crying in Coleen's arms. The sisters' conversation revealed that Conrad Wooten was undoubtedly the reason for her distress.

"Oh, Ruthie, you have to tell Daddy. Next time, he won't stop with a pinch or a feel. He'll force you all the way."

"I know, Coleen. The very sight of him makes me sick to my stomach. But he threatened to hurt Daddy and throw us out if I tell. Daddy and Mommy can't know."

For the victims of Jim Crow racism, each demeaning encounter tightened the yoke of fear and helplessness. Such had been the sisters' reality since they had come of age.

But something on the inside would rise up in Ruth that day. In the midst of her circumstance, Nate and Mamie's first born was given vision to see beyond the visible. She sat straight up, turning her lovely eyes to Coleen. A defiant resolve shone through the tears.

"My body will be a gift to my husband when I marry. No one is going to take it by force."

From that day on, Luke watched over his sisters like a hawk. He pledged to be there, ready to defend them with his life.

It wasn't long before Conrad struck again. Nate and Mamie had started out for town on foot that morning. It would be a while before they returned. The girls' employer released them early, so Luke was not there to walk them home. He was stacking wood out back when Coleen came screaming, her pretty face bloodied and terrified.

"Oh, Luke, Conrad Wooten pulled Ruthie into his truck. I tried to stop him but he kicked me down and drove off towards the woods."

Luke prayed for mercy as he raced to his sister, tracking them down in short order. The truck was partially concealed by a patch of high grass. The grace of God was already at work as he reached the scene. Ruthie was calling Jesus while her abuser was trying in vain to curse whom God had blessed. But try as he might, Conrad was unable to perform.

Just as he lifted his fist to silence her supplication, Luke seized his sister's would be rapist from the truck and the two struggled on the ground. Conrad snarled his contempt for the colored boy who dared to oppose him.

"It was a pleasure to sire you boy, and it will be my pleasure to take you out of here. When I'm finished with your sister, just consider your worthless days numbered!"

Then, suddenly, a gunshot rang out. Conrad Wooten fell dead across the son he'd discarded before his birth. Luke now found himself face-to-face with the grimacing, open-eyed corpse of his oppressor. Horrified and repulsed, he turned away just in time to see Mrs. Lilith Wooten turn the weapon on herself.

The murder-suicide of Waylow, Mississippi's most prominent and powerful couple had been witnessed by two of its most vulnerable citizens.

Luke, though innocent, had not only wrestled with Conrad but his clothes were also stained with the dead man's blood. Jim Crow law would hold him accountable. A colored man had no right to defend himself or his family against a white man. In coming to his sister's rescue, Luke had done the unthinkable and survived.

After rolling Conrad's body aside, he stood up and made his way to his sister. Ruthie's trembling hands were trying in vain to pull up her ripped panties. Luke tenderly helped her from the truck.

Shock and adrenaline urged the two siblings forward until they made their way home to Coleen, who had bandaged her own wound, and filled the tin tub for her sister.

While Luke washed up from a basin, Coleen gently bathed Ruthie who recited the sordid details as if in a dream. The two girls then burned the bloody clothing.

By the time their parents returned, Luke had packed his few belongings. Nate and Mamie listened with heavy hearts as their son told the story. They all knew he could not remain and hope to stay alive.

Mamie went over to the dresser and pulled out a Bible. Too

distraught for words, she kissed her son on both cheeks, pressing the Book to his chest.

"Are you sure, Momma?"

Mamie nodded her assurance and began to weep for the son she might never see again. Luke thanked his mother before placing the family heirloom in his sack.

Nate came forward and embraced Luke, holding him tightly. Then, led by the Spirit, he laid hands on his only son, declaring again that prophecy spoken just a few weeks ago. Finally, Nate kissed his forehead and released him with a blessing.

"Go with God, son. I love you."

Colleen and Ruth pressed the dollars they'd managed to save into his pockets. As Luke turned for the door, the two young women fell on their brother in unison. In contrite repentance for the years of sibling affection withheld, they showered him with tearful hugs and kisses.

The very moment Luke received his family's unrestrained affection he would have to leave it all behind. He took off into the night blinded by his own tears.

The path Luke would assume as he departed Waylow, would hold him captive until the appointed time. Throughout those years, a bleak isolation reigned, born of the lie.

But he never sank low enough to abandon the hope that fueled his survival. By grace he battled despair, believing that one day there'd be a reckoning, if his people could just hold on.

❋ ❋ ❋ ❋ ❋ ❋

When the telling of his story ended, neither Luke nor Dana recalled how they had come to join hands. They sat very still, as if holding on for dear life.

Finally Luke spoke.

"Dana, I didn't set out to pass for white. I never found my coloring any cause for celebration. But, it didn't take long for a frightened teenage runaway to learn that passing would make it easier to stay alive and earn a living.

By the time I made it up to D.C. and finally into New York, I'd gotten really good at playing the role.

In time, I earned my high school diploma and then began working toward a two year degree at night.

One day, during my lunch break, I spotted a casting call flyer for a local play. Responding to that audition marked the beginning of my transition from janitor to thespian. I was already a walking fabrication so why not earn a living at it?

I moved among white people like a Trojan horse without a cause. And, I tried to be as cold and heartless to their women as Conrad had been to mine.

But there was one exception – the women gave themselves to me willingly, convinced that I was making love to them. I'd gotten pretty good at that pretense too. A part of me enjoyed taking advantage of their ignorance even as the lie sullied my heart and soul."

Luke smiled sadly and his voice began to crack.

"I recently made contact with my former pastor who told me that my parents had passed. He said they grew old before their time – too much heartache and sorrow. He didn't know what happened to my sisters after they moved away.

Dana, I didn't even attend my own parents' funerals. I have no idea if my sisters are dead or alive. I ran for my life and left them behind. And I've been running from the truth ever since."

Luke cupped Dana's hand to his chest, as if to soothe the pain that had ravaged his heart for so long. Teal colored eyes searched her face, pleading. Ebony eyes responded with loving compassion. Then the dam broke and Luke dropped his head onto Dana's lap. His tears soaked her skirt but she was not concerned. This was her intended, and no one was mad but the devil.

Meanwhile, back on Halsey Street, Kitty watched Isaac as he watched the clock and found excuses to stay up. She made fish Po'boys that neither of them ate. Then, they played a game of Scrabble that nobody won.

"Kitty, what exactly did Dana say before she left?"

"She said that she needed to see Luke. Then she called Melvin and asked to borrow his car."

"But Luke was just here for dinner."

"Well, maybe she needed to see him alone. Dana is a grown woman."

"I know that, baby, but this is not like her."

"Well, your sister has never really been in love before."

Realizing that her comment did nothing to ease Isaac's concern, Kitty gently added, "Honey, we have to trust that they are submitted to Jesus. And now I think it's time for us to turn in."

After they prayed, Kitty watched her husband's profile as he stared at the bedroom ceiling.

He kept thinking that his baby sister was alone with this white guy in his Greenwich Village studio! Although Isaac hated to go there, Luke's torrid past flooded his mind.

In silence he sought the Lord. *Father, where are you in this?*

After a time, that still, small voice spoke to his heart. *The same God that kept you is able to keep them.*

Soon after, Isaac dozed off into a light slumber, and Kitty followed.

Then, around 3:00 am they were awakened by voices and went downstairs. Dana had returned bringing Luke with her. Both of them were swollen eyed and slightly disheveled.

Kitty spoke first, "What on earth …?"

Luke stared at the floor, grateful for Dana's quick reply. "Sorry to worry you guys, we're fine – just tired."

Kitty met her husband's eyes, hugged the weary pair and went back to bed.

Dana kissed her brother softly and proceeded to her room. Luke watched lovingly as she disappeared up the stairs, and then turned to face her brother.

The two men were left alone in the foyer. For a moment, they stood there, reading each other. A silent exchange ensued wherein Isaac asked the question that Luke answered to his satisfaction.

Then Dana's brother spoke. "Tomorrow's another day. Let's all get some sleep."

Luke went to the guest room, at peace with his surroundings. He slept-in past morning. The Walkers did not disturb him when they rose for breakfast. Sometime past noon he awoke with a joyful heart. A burden had been lifted and, for the first time in his adult life, Luke felt free.

After dressing, lunch was calling his name. He came downstairs to feast on smothered chops, butter beans, and red rice, kept warm for him in the oven.

Later that day, Isaac and Luke would have their own conversation on the stoop.

As they sat together watching the sights, it went like this between the brothers.

"So, Dana tells me that you're colored."

"Yep, I'm colored."

"Are you sure you're not *Calling those things that are not as though they were*? Because quiet as it's kept, *God* does that."

"No, man, I'm colored!"

"Okay, well, you know I love you, man."

"I know, and I love you too, Isaac."

"And, I believe that you and Dana are in love."

"Yes, we are, very much so."

Isaac turned to face his best friend. Luke met his gaze.

"Now, Luke, if you hurt my sister I'm going to lay my religion down and come after you. I'll just have to repent later."

"Well, Isaac, I wouldn't blame any man for defending his sister. But you won't have to."

A brief silence ensued.

"Well, alright then, welcome to the family, man."

"Thanks, man."

Dana and Kitty, who'd been watching them from the parlor floor window, breathed a sigh of relief when the two men shook hands, slapped backs, and then fell out laughing.

In the end, every word declared to young Luke by his future father-in-law, would come to pass. At the time the prophecy was given, no one could have imagined just how it would unfold.

But that didn't matter. All our God requires is faith and obedience at the appointed time. And Jesus provides grace for that as He works in us to will and to do according to His good purpose.

By 1963, the nation's growing pains were a force to be reckoned with – terrible and wonderful all at once. Luke and Isaac, like the characters they'd portrayed on stage, had formed an enduring friendship in the midst of adversity. These two men and the women they loved would not be idle spectators in the movement that was about to explode. They were destined for the front line.

After following the news reports and seeking God's will, they felt called to Mississippi. Unsure of where to start, Kitty reached out to the NAACP, who put her in contact with two devoted freedom workers. A school teacher, named Ruth Kelly, and a registered nurse, named Coleen Black, would be their hosts in Jackson.

Luke's emotional reunion with his sisters would take place in the trenches of the civil rights movement.

But, there'd be one crucial stop on their journey down South.

Before daybreak, on the morning of August 28, 1963, Luke, Dana, Isaac and Kitty departed Brooklyn for Harlem, where they'd set out to attend the March on Washington. From that gathering place, hundreds of buses would leave the city en route to our nation's capital.

Dana Prince boarded the bus and sat down with her husband, ignoring the stares of onlookers. At first glance Dana and Luke appeared to be the personification of interracial love: rare, curious, and sometimes...aloof. But before long the couple's interaction with Isaac and Kitty put everyone at ease.

By the time Luke's ethnicity was made known it no longer mattered to anyone. The love of God had knit those freedom riders together as they traveled into history.

Just as the caravan of buses began to emerge from the Baltimore Harbor Tunnel, Luke's baby kicked in Dana's womb for the first time – a sign of new life and hope for the future.

Not the End

Sifting the Squeeze

"Simon, Simon, Satan has asked to sift all of you as
wheat. But I have prayed for you, Simon,
that your faith may not fail. And when you have
turned back, strengthen your brothers.
~Luke 22: 31-32

Sifting the Squeeze

It was Women's Day at Living Word Fellowship Church. Needless to say, the choir was off the chain. But Tyra Redding's praise had been in a steady decline for months. Standing in the sanctuary with hands lifted, she recalled the time when God's presence comforted her like a warm embrace.

Now, as she tearfully sought His face, the Father's response felt more like the loving conviction due a wayward child.

Still, Tyra was not ready to submit. Her heart was ensnared by the one she'd mistaken for an answered prayer. Looking across the aisle to where Wilson Yearwood sat, she found it hard to believe they'd been together just a few hours ago.

Wilson's departure from her condo the night before followed the same routine. As they stood in the doorway, Tyra made the familiar appeal, hoping in vain for a different response.

"Wilson, will you sit with me in church tomorrow?"

And, true to form, the darkness that feigned light refused her once again.

"Baby, I know it must seem selfish of me, but I don't want to expose this precious thing we have to those who are too self-righteous to understand."

Wilson lifted her chin ever so gently. Then, from a heart void of compassion, his lying words continued.

"Tyra, I don't want people thinking less of you than they should. Listen, when the time is right, our public announcement will be the rock I'll place on your finger. That's a promise."

So smooth was his rejection, Tyra almost asked him to forgive her request. Instead, she lovingly buttoned his coat and stood on her tip-toes to turn up his collar.

"You take such good care of me. I'm one blessed man! See you tomorrow, my love."

Wilson departed with a tender kiss, leaving her alone. Tyra would not bathe until morning, longing to keep his scent with her as long as possible. She'd use whatever remained of his presence to fight her mounting fear and insecurity. Crawling between the tousled sheets, Tyra prayed to the One who truly loved her.

"Lord, I feel as if my life has been turned upside down. But, I love him so. Please let this work out for me."

Tyra awoke Sunday morning, still clinging to the pillow where his head had been. Before she left for the 11:00 o'clock service, Wilson's favorite Sunday meal would be carefully prepared by his soul-tied captive.

He'd come by after church to feast on braised ox tails, peas and rice, and cabbage cooked with smoked meat. Tyra would be dessert.

However, despite her lavish outpouring of affection, Wilson rarely spent the night. He'd convinced Tyra that his staying over on a regular basis would cheapen their relationship.

"Too much like shacking," he would say. He felt they should leave some things for marriage.

And so, having received what he'd come for, Wilson made his excuses. "Baby, it's so hard to say goodnight, but Monday mornings are crazy for me. Dinner was fabulous as always. I'll call you tomorrow."

"Okay, Wilson, I love you."

"I love you more," he replied. And he was gone.

Back at his bachelor pad, Wilson praised Tyra to the four walls and proclaimed her virtues out loud.

"My woman is the gift that keeps on giving! She has let me in to places where no man has gone before. Rare is the man who can say that about his main squeeze."

Indeed, Tyra was a special prize. It had been years since he'd had a virgin. Even in the church, they were hard to find. For that reason alone, Tyra was a keeper. And Wilson was determined to keep her, as long as she respected his space.

He'd walked away from many women over this issue. However, Wilson took great pride in the fact that no woman had ever walked away from him!

Not one of his conquests ever managed to pinpoint the source of his power to captivate. Although he lacked the traditional pretty boy features, Wilson's appeal was hard to resist.

He began shaving his head in high school, at the first sign of a receding hairline. His caramel colored skin was slightly scarred by teenage acne, but no one seemed to notice.

During his freshman year in college, a jealous husband cracked his two front teeth. As a result, Wilson's smile was upgraded to a complete porcelain makeover, compliments of the man's love-sick, cheating wife.

At 5 feet 6 inches, Wilson favored petite women, who were no threat to his modest stature. He was stocky by nature, but regular trips to the gym kept his weight under control. His dress was conservative, straight out of a Brooks Brothers catalog.

He sought to be taken seriously, not only by his business associates, but by the women who brought him pleasure. On the surface, Wilson appeared safe, successful, and full of promise.

Wilson's childhood, however, had been filled with all the sights and sounds of a low income, latch-key kid. The most pivotal experience of his youth had been his father's abandonment of the family.

Tobias Yearwood was offered the opportunity to become a fulltime kept man. It was just too good to pass up. On the day he walked out, six-year-old Wilson had to be pried away from his undeserving hero.

"Okay, my man, you're too old for tears. Daddy has to leave, so go to your mother. Sallie, take the boy!"

Meanwhile, Wilson's sister, Tina, refused their father's goodbye kiss. "Just like your momma," was all he said, when Tina ran from his embrace.

Then Tobias bid farewell to the wife he'd long since grown tired of. "I guess you knew this day was coming, Sallie. I never pretended to be a family man."

"No, Toby, you just pretended to be a man. God help you."

Tobias shook his head and looked her up and down.

"Baby, you're one wreck of a woman, downright impossible to live with. Listen, you and your God take care of my kids. I'm through."

With that, Tobias walked out the door. As the sound of his footsteps faded from the stairwell, Sallie went over to the front window. She saw her husband's older woman reach across the front seat to unlock the Lincoln Town Car. Mr. Yearwood put his bags in the trunk and slipped behind the wheel of his most recent gift. In seconds, he was gone.

The two siblings watched as their mother took a seat and

continued to stare out the window. About a half hour later Sallie abandoned her vigil, entered the bedroom where her children were conceived, and shut the door.

What now, Lord? What shall I do?

From her purse, Sallie pulled out a dog-eared business card. In bold letters surrounded by a black and white ethnic print border, it read, *Kitty Walker, Attorney at Law*.

Sallie's best friend, Marta, was a paralegal for the Walker law firm. She'd begged Sallie for years to take action regarding Tobias' neglect. Staring down at the card, she recalled their last conversation.

"Marta, I know you mean well, but I haven't given up on my marriage. Toby's never gone for more than a few days."

"Sallie, that's only because his clothes are still there. But one day he'll pack up for good. Then where will you be? Like the old folks used to say, you need to prepare for war in the time of peace."

"I don't have money for any lawyer."

"A consultation won't cost you anything. Ms. Walker will work with you. She's not your average attorney. She's been an advocate for the disenfranchised since the 1960s. Sallie, at least talk to her about your options. You owe it to yourself and your children."

"God hates divorce, Marta. I want to be in His will."

"Sallie, God hates adultery too. And I'm sure he hates what these STDs are doing to your body. At least give it some thought. I'm with you, whatever you decide."

A week after that conversation, Marta's words had come to pass. Looking around at the ransacked drawers and piles of empty hangers, Sallie felt the walls closing in on her. It was too much to handle at that moment.

Tomorrow, I'll sort things out. Right now my babies need their dinner.

That evening, she sat her two fatherless tykes down to meatloaf, mashed potatoes, and green peas. The trio then snuggled together to watch *The Cosby Show,* each of them longing to change places with a Huxtable.

After a long, restless night, Sallie rose to face her first day as a single mom.

When the dust cleared, all Tobias had left behind was a half used bottle of Brute cologne. Sallie threw it in the trash, but she kept silent when she saw Wilson retrieve it. He treasured that meager token of his father's existence. It would be the only scent worn by Wilson, for most of his life.

Sallie never called the lawyer. Hoping in vain for her husband's return, she worked two jobs to raise her children. She saw them through college and prayed diligently for their souls, even as the world pulled against her efforts. But when Sallie went home to Jesus, her prayers had not been answered.

Wilson's favorite night spot was called The Gentlemen's Agreement. Twice a week, he joined the pack of well-dressed businessmen that entered solo, but never left that way. It was speed dating for consenting adults, and there was no shortage of women to choose from.

These women came wanting to be taken. In giving themselves to the takers, they hoped to dispel their loneliness, if only for a night. Wilson and his predatory brethren sensed their desperation like dogs in heat. And, they were more than happy to oblige.

But, things were not that simple when it came to Wilson's main squeeze. This area of his love life brought him much tribulation. No matter how good he treated his main squeeze of the moment, she became clingy after a while.

Eventually, the pressure would begin to set a wedding date. Bridal magazines and ads for engagement rings would start appearing on the bed. Then, she'd start asking him to account for his absences. That behavior always forced Wilson to move on.

As a CPA and statistician, Wilson's life was all about the numbers. "Just follow the numbers. The numbers determine your course of action," he'd proclaim to his image in the mirror.

This principle served him not only in business, but in his private affairs as well. Wilson viewed his love life as the logical end product of the male-to-female ratio.

He believed that given the shortage of eligible bachelors, no man should be expected to limit himself to the bondage of monogamy. It was insane for women to expect such a thing.

But, because he felt that the weaker sex was not capable of handling this reality, he never tried to enlighten them.

Wilson further believed that most men desired his lifestyle, but they weren't honest enough to face it. And, the few that did walk-the-walk, were entirely too competitive, as if there weren't enough women to go around!

As a result, Wilson kept his own counsel and had few male friends. His BFF was the man in the mirror. In preaching to this one-man choir, Wilson had perfected the art of self-delusion.

Once, he tried to share his beliefs at the Yearwood's annual reunion/barbeque. Wilson showed up that year with a particular target audience in mind. It was only logical to assume that the raging hormones of his younger male relatives would make them especially open to the message.

And so, while engaging his potential disciples in a game of hoops, Wilson began to preach.

"Listen and learn my brothers! The male-to-female ratio is the foundation for determining your relationships with the opposite sex. Once you embrace the reality of those numbers, the rest is conversation.

Never underestimate the power of words. Sow the right words, and the possibilities are endless. I'm a witness; the right words can reap a harvest of blessings and take you anywhere you want to go, if you know what I mean."

Unfortunately for Wilson, there were other men in attendance that did not share his point of view. Nor did they appreciate his particular brand of evangelism.

Needless to say, a heated argument ensued. It quickly got down to a virtual tug of war for the soul of the next generation. Eventually, Wilson was asked to either shut up or stay away.

He decided to do the latter. But that rejection only served to convince him that he was one of a few brave men honest enough to follow the only reasonable, albeit narrow, path.

Of course, Wilson embraced the idea of a man's right to have it both ways. In spite of his perpetual womanizing, he felt that certain comforts of married life were essential to his wellbeing. And he was quite capable of enjoying those comforts, while remaining single. All it took was a woman willing to settle for less than God's best.

With the abundance of such women at his disposal, Wilson rarely found himself without a main squeeze. His main squeeze was the steady rock that sustained him, as he tossed and turned on the waves of one night stands.

He'd discovered some time ago that the church was the best hunting ground for a main squeeze. If Wilson could get hold of a church-going woman before she was submitted to Jesus, he'd have Susie Homemaker, on demand. Many of these women were on a mission to prove how good a help-meet they could be.

In return Wilson embraced the principle of just rewards. Because this woman gave him more than physical benefits, he reasoned that she should receive more, as well.

Therefore, any woman considered by Wilson to be his main squeeze, was sure to receive more time, attention, and deception, than all of his one night stands put together.

He went to great lengths to secure his main squeeze. In addition to the false promise of marriage, there were all kinds of crafty firewalls in place to protect her from the hurtful reality of his double life. He even had a separate phone line for her exclusive access to him. Needless to say, he alone managed the availability of access at any given time.

Although they were high maintenance, Wilson never walked away from his main squeeze, until she made it impossible for him to stay.

Soon after his last break-up, just prior to meeting Tyra, Wilson was taking it pretty hard. When his solitary efforts at self-encouragement failed, he turned to his sister. Seeking comfort from Tina was an act of insanity, but Wilson was desperate.

And, in a startling departure from his usual decorum, Wilson was also slightly drunk.

After several rounds at a local bar, he showed up at Tina's door and started banging. When that didn't rouse her, he leaned on the doorbell, nonstop. That worked. Tina jumped up out of a deep sleep, grabbed her pistol from the nightstand and went to the door.

After checking the peep hole, she let Wilson in, to the tune of a pissed-off, Cushite, tirade.

"Negro, don't you ever come to my door like that again. You must have forgotten where you are. What's up with you?"

"Sorry Sis, I need to talk."

"Well, you picked a fine time to go slumming. I work hard and I need my rest."

The two siblings entered Tina's hot pink living room and sat down on her leopard print sofa.

Tina was one of the few people that made Wilson nervous. He thrived on his ability to deceive women, and she saw right through him. Even now, he couldn't look her in the eye.

But, having nowhere else to go, Wilson wrung his hands, and began his attempt to cry on her ice-cold shoulder.

"Tina, you're a woman, right?"

"Last time I looked, I was. My customers at Club 4-Play seem to agree. What's your problem, big brother?"

Wilson lifted his bloodshot eyes just long enough to see Tina light a cigarette and cross her killer legs.

"Well, Sis, my problem is that I'm being persecuted, because I just can't bring myself to give women something they really don't want."

Tina exhaled. Her eyes followed the trail of smoke to the ceiling.

"Uh huh, and just what is it that women really don't want that you can't bring yourself to give?"

"Now hear me out, okay?"

"I'm listening, Wilson."

"Well Tina, women don't want the truth. So I don't give it to them. Instead, I tell them what makes them feel good, what their tender hearts long to hear. Listen, it's not my fault that there's so many women, and so few men to go around.

I see it this way. I didn't create this ratio. I just make the most of the hand I've been dealt. All things considered, I'm a numbers man."

Once more, Wilson forced himself to look over at Tina, but her expression caused him to turn away. He resumed his appeal.

"It's this unrealistic monogamy thing that keeps men like me from being transparent in relationships. And that always ends in tragedy for me, and for the woman I'm in love with, at the time."

Wilson waited for a response from his sister. But, none came. So, he continued to plead his case.

"You know something else?"

"No, tell me, Wilson."

"Okay, here's another revelation. There's one religious group that seems to have it somewhat right. But, as fate would have it, their women just don't appeal to me.

They cover themselves behind long dresses and veils, calling on a deity that would refuse a brother his spare ribs and pork chops! No way can I deal with that. Besides, Momma would roll over in her grave."

The absurdity of Wilson's last comment did not escape Tina.

"Wilson, considering the lives we're living, I'm pretty sure Momma is already rolling."

Wilson grabbed his bald head, utterly exasperated.

"Tina...Tina...you know what I mean!"

He shut his eyes for a second in order to better concentrate. Then, pointing to himself, he declared in a loud voice, "I have to stick with the Jesus crowd!"

"I see," said Tina.

"Do you really, Tina? Listen, even modest church attire gives a brother some inkling of what the women have to work with, underneath. The moral codes are not as strict – at least in practice. The diet is more to my liking, and Tina, you just got to give Gospel music its due.

So yeah, it's the Jesus crowd for me. All things considered, I want a saved woman for my main squeeze!"

"Stop right there. I need a drink."

Tina rose and went over to her fully loaded bar. She returned with two glasses of Johnny Walker Black. Wilson received the cup with gladness.

"Please continue," Tina mumbled, as she lit another cigarette from the stub.

"Well, in case you haven't guessed it by now, I had to leave Pamela. She had become impossible.

But, these break-ups are killing me. Sis, my double life is taking a toll. I just can't understand why women think they're the only ones that hurt when it's all over. Just look at me. I'm slightly drunk, when last have you seen me slightly drunk?"

It was true that Tina hadn't seen her brother under the influence since high school. But, not caring enough to voice any agreement with him, she kept silent. And so, Wilson continued.

"Here's the bottom line, I can't survive without a main squeeze. I've got to have someone to love and care for me.

But, there are certain puzzlements that I struggle with. Maybe you can shed some light, being that you're a woman."

"I'm still listening, big brother."

"Okay, here we go. Tina, just why do they insist on marriage? What's so special about a ring and a license? And furthermore, why can't they understand that the booty calls mean nothing? Listen, a million one night stands can't take away my love for my main squeeze. Tina, I'm so misunderstood!"

With those final remarks, Wilson threw up his hands to announce the end of his plea. He sighed heavily, as if exhausted from the effort. Then, he looked over at the bar.

"Tina, may I please refresh my drink?"

"Help yourself."

After refilling his glass, Wilson made his way back to the sofa. Then he sat down and began to cry.

Tina observed her brother with practiced detachment, as he wept into his drink. She had no compassion to give.

In a few short hours, her body would be groping a pole for the pleasure of his kind. After five years as an exotic dancer, her low opinion of men was exceeded only by her own degree of self-loathing.

But, right now what Tina wanted most was sleep.

She muttered under her breath, "Just like our father. Where do I even begin with this fool?"

"What did you say, Sis? I didn't hear you."

"I'm just thinking out loud, big brother."

Tina got up and refilled her glass. Then, from her perch on a bar stool, she looked down at Wilson, and began her rebuttal.

"Wilson, you do keep life insurance, correct?"

Wilson looked up from his drink in total bewilderment. Johnny Walker had kicked in enough to season his next words with an air of indignation.

"What! I'm here pouring my heart and soul out to you, and you're asking about life insurance? Of course, I keep life insurance. I'm a numbers man!"

"I'm very glad. Because one day somebody's going to find your sorry behind dead and castrated by one of these women you've been messing over. And I don't want to have to go around taking up collections for your burial fund.

Now, I've heard enough. You can either get your slightly-drunk tail out of my house, or you can crash on the couch. But, whatever you do, I'm going back to bed!"

Wilson made his way home that night, speaking words of comfort to his twisted mind.

"In my time of need all I could get from my closest living relative is a death wish. She's jealous and incapable of reasoning. Just because I did something with my college degree while she's wasting hers as a stripper!

She's a hater, like the rest of my family. Well, I've passed this way before. I just need to pull myself together. I must be slipping, letting some female get to me this way. I'm a numbers man and the numbers are on my side!

Just wait, Wilson Yearwood is going to have a new squeeze, very soon. You got that? I hope you heard that, Tina."

Wilson would require a few days of recuperation before going back on the prowl.

✱✱✱✱✱✱

Most of Tyra's 30 years had been spent in pursuit of an education and a career. She'd done things in the prescribed order, putting first things first. From her wish list, she'd checked off the well-paying job and the condo. After landing a position as a pediatric nurse practitioner, Tyra bought a place that could rival anything on HGTV.

Sadly, on the heels of those accomplishments came Tyra's

devastating loss of both parents. Milton and Clara Redding departed this world while vacationing in Florida. Their rental boat capsized in rough waters.

Tyra had always attended church with them, in keeping with family tradition. But, after their passing, she joined Living Word Fellowship, where Pastor Kevin Bush drew a younger congregation. There, Tyra hoped to improve her chances for marriage.

Just a few months into Tyra's new membership, the ministry began to speak to her situation.

Having returned from a leadership seminar on church growth, Pastor Bush announced that he'd received a divine revelation. His new assignment was to teach the flock how to faithfully stand on the promises of God.

It would involve a two-step process. First, each member was to sow a series of financial seeds. Then for those who were obedient in their sowing, Pastor Bush would declare a corporate fast that would usher them into a new level of blessings.

Tyra clung to her pastor's every word. She desperately wanted God to send her a mate and was therefore glad to sow her seeds.

Unfortunately, Tyra wasn't taught the importance of delighting oneself in the Lord, so that her desires would be in keeping with His will. As a result, the corporate fast was merely the culmination of her efforts to get a husband, pure and simple.

Her obsession with finding the man she thought would complete her life, had left her vulnerable to deception, and destined for heartache. Wilson walked into Tyra's life on the final day of her fast.

"Is this seat taken, woman of God?" Wilson crooned as he approached Tyra on the Flatbush Avenue bus. She looked up from her *Daily Bread* into a smile that rocked her world.

"Why, yes, of course – I mean no, it's not taken." Tyra replied, as she gathered her belongings to make room for him.

"I've never been called a woman of God before, but it sounds nice. Thank you!"

Wilson sat down, and went to work.

"You're very welcome. However, I only speak what I see. And I see virtue all over you, my sister. By the way, I'm Wilson – Wilson Yearwood. May I ask your name?"

"Oh, yes, I'm Tyra Redding."

"Well, it's a pleasure to finally meet you, Tyra Redding."

"Finally meet me? I don't understand."

The player put on a bashful grin. He even managed to blush.

"Tyra … I must confess that I've been watching you on this bus for some time now."

"You have?" Tyra replied, blushing for real.

"Yes, indeed. I've noticed that you're always reading the Bible, or something inspirational. I think that's awesome. By the way, where do you go to church?"

"I attend Living Word Fellowship, over on Eastern Parkway."

That's very good, thought Wilson. He'd never preyed there before.

"Wow, I've caught your service online; your choir is amazing – Pastor Kevin Bush, right?"

"Yes, that's correct. What church do you attend?"

"Actually, I'm between churches, at the moment. I've been praying about a church home for a while. You know Tyra, the Lord works in mysterious ways."

"Indeed He does. And Wilson, I can testify that Living Word will surely bless you."

Again, Wilson's response was strategic and effective.

"Oh, I'm feeling blessed right now! This may just be an answer to my prayers."

Tyra couldn't help but wonder if this was the answer to her prayers as well.

Then Wilson reached over and shook her hand.

"Tyra, it's been a pleasure."

It was more than a handshake; the contact was ecstatic. Tyra's heart raced, and her stomach was queasy. She couldn't stop smiling.

Oh Lord, she thought, *please let him come to Living Word this Sunday.*

Not knowing what to say or do next, Tyra withdrew her hand (reluctantly) and began to fumble in her purse for a business card.

But, just then, Wilson rang the bell and stood up to leave.

"This is my stop. I hope to see you again, Tyra. Have a blessed weekend."

"Me too, and you be blessed as well!"

Wow, thought Tyra, *he thinks it's awesome that I read God's word. Surely that's a good sign!*

And so, Cupid's fiery dart had been planted. The wolf had found his next prey, in a believer who had yet to be sifted.

Wilson had made himself known to Tyra after five days of strategic reconnaissance. Now, having found his mark, he was beside himself, with the promise of new pleasures and comforts. The monotonous diet of casual sex was never enough to fulfill his needs.

He lay in bed that night, smiling in remembrance of their conversation. Wilson testified to the ceiling, "Lovely Tyra is mine. Yes indeed, I'll have exclusive access to her bed and an honored place at her table in no time."

It had been a month since his breakup with Pamela.

After Tyra's conversation with Wilson, she walked home from the bus stop in a daze. She entered her condo and went straight to the spa shower. As the pulsating massage soothed away all the cares of her workday, Tyra began to unwind. The thought of Wilson put her over the moon. It seemed that everything she wanted was falling into place.

Wow, she thought, *God has sent me a man before my fast even ended. Well, why not? Haven't I done everything my pastor said?*

Tyra stepped out of the shower and stood before the full length mirror. Proportionately distributed over her 4 foot 11 inch frame, were 115 pounds of pure, unadulterated flesh. She was a well-toned, size 4.

Tyra's Master's degree in nursing provided her with lots of knowledge regarding the human body and how it functioned. She'd always been confident that marriage to the right man, along with her clinical information, was all she'd need for a glorious wedding night. But for the first time, as Tyra faced her image in the mirror, a cloud came over her mind.

If Wilson is the one, will he like me? Will I please him?

Suddenly, her utmost concern was to gain the acceptance of a man she knew nothing about. She was anxious and excited all at once. In her giddiness, there was no peace. But, Tyra didn't notice.

Tyra began to take a mental inventory of her assets. She was confident that her home was ready to host any honored guest. But, she would need a personal make-over.

She slipped into her pajamas and went over to the walk-in closet. It was filled, for the most part, with medical scrubs.

Okay, I need some new clothes. I don't even know what to buy. She turned on her T.V. and set the DVR to record *What Not to Wear*.

Tyra remembered watching that show at her cousin, Abby's house. Abby and Aunt Jean were the fashionistas in the family.

In fact, that branch of the Redding clan owned a string of full service day spas called RenewVation. Tyra couldn't recall the last time she'd treated herself to a day spa experience.

I'm overdue, Tyra thought, as she grabbed the phone. Abby answered after the first ring.

"Thank you for calling RenewVation. This is Abby. How may I

serve you today?"

"Hey Cuz, what's up?"

"Hey there, Ty. Girl, Mommy was just asking about you."

"Oh, please tell Aunt Jean I'm coming over real soon. I've been working hard for the money. But, I love my job."

"Well, you're a natural caregiver. Children's Hospital is blessed to have you."

"Yeah, but now the caregiver could use some personal care. Abby, I'm calling for a spa appointment. I know Saturdays are very busy, but could you possibly fit me in?"

"No worries girl, you're family. Let's see, can you be here by 8:00 am?"

"That's perfect, thanks so much, Abby."

"My pleasure, what are you having done?"

"Okay, besides the full body massage, I'd like a manicure and pedicure. I could use a new hair style. And I'd like to try a little make-up. Listen Cuz, just give me the works."

"No problem…and we'll talk later on, yes?"

"What do you mean?"

"I mean, who is he?"

"Girl, stop!"

"Don't 'girl, stop' me!"

"Okay Abby, love you."

"Love you too. See you in the morning."

Tyra hung up the phone and smiled herself to sleep.

Although Abby Redding was a master cosmetologist and registered masseuse, it had been a while since she'd functioned in those capacities. The duties of management kept her away from the hands on operations.

But, today would be an exception. Her cousin was going to receive a head to toe make-over, with Abby at the helm.

When Tyra walked into the lobby of RenewVation's flagship location, Abby was at the door to personally greet her. She had been itching to enhance Tyra's natural beauty for some time.

"Well Ty, are you ready to see yourself magnified?"

"I am, indeed. Let's get started."

As she led Tyra to the back, Abby reminded her brother, Josh, that she'd be tied up the whole day.

"No problem, I have it, Sis. Go take care of our cousin."

Abby was more than a little curious about her cousin's sudden desire for a make-over. However, to her surprise, Tyra was not ready to discuss the matter.

"Abby, it's really nothing to tell at this point; I just want to be prepared. We'll talk later, okay?"

Abby wasn't sure how to read between the lines of her cousin's words. But she wasn't led to push the issue.

"Okay Ty, as long as you're happy."

Like most of the Redding clan, Tyra's coloring was rich copper with ruddy undertones. Her late dad, Milton, and his twin brother Will, traced their ancestry back to the Seminole people. Tyra's high cheek bones and long black hair seemed to corroborate their claim. Abby's brother, Josh was the spitting image of his father, Will.

On the other hand, Jean Redding had passed her fair skin and light hair on to Abby. When the three cousins were growing up, Tyra and Josh were often mistaken for the siblings. Abby had envied Tyra's darker-toned beauty throughout their childhood.

But, all that changed as Abby came to know the love of God. Self-acceptance was just one of the blessings that followed. Last year, at her 30th birthday celebration, Abby's golden Sister Locks had grown to waist length. In a suede wrap dress and platform ankle boots, she rocked a mix of vintage soul and modern flair.

Abby and her team of stylists had helped many of RenewVation's clients find their own fashion sense. She'd do no less for Tyra.

At the end of her spa experience, Tyra's body felt great, and she had a striking new look. Her hair had been blown straight and cut into a bi-level style. The Cleopatra inspired look enhanced Tyra's almond shaped eyes and gorgeous cheekbones.

RenewVation had its own cosmetics line, called Pure Grace. From that signature collection, Abby created a natural looking make-up palette that Tyra could easily accomplish for herself at home.

Needless to say, Tyra was overjoyed when Abby handed her the mirror.

"Wow, I didn't know I could look this good!"

"Ty, it was easy, considering all I had to work with."

Tyra missed the compliment, as her mind flashed back to her clothes closet.

"Now I need to do something about my wardrobe, or the lack thereof."

"Ty, I'm way ahead of you. How about we take a little shopping trip? Josh has things under control here."

"Thanks so much Cuz. I actually feel like a princess."

Abby hugged her cousin and thought to herself, *I sure hope he turns out to be a prince!*

Over the next few hours, they hit several neighborhood boutiques. That evening, Tyra went home with the all the basic pieces needed to look tastefully chic, whenever she was out of uniform.

Tyra awoke the next morning for church, like it was the first day of school. She had laid her clothes out before going to bed. The ten minute make-up routine went surprisingly well, for her first attempt. Her hair unwrapped and fell into place, with very little effort. Finally, Tyra stepped into a coral and fuchsia color block dress. Nude patent pumps, and a quilted satchel completed the look.

By the time Tyra reached Living Word Fellowship, she had received all kinds of positive feedback from men and women on the street. The wallflower had become a butterfly, overnight. She kept reassuring herself that this new visibility thing was okay.

The sanctuary at Living Word was not very large. Tyra usually sat toward the front, as not to be distracted during worship. But, this Sunday, she positioned herself on the last row. From there, she could look for Wilson, without having to turn around.

A few minutes after Tyra sat down, Wilson walked in. He wore a dark navy pinstripe suit, and a burgundy foulard tie. Having no intension of sitting with Tyra, he allowed the usher to direct him to a seat.

He didn't look for her. There was no need to; he knew she'd be looking for him. Wilson could feel Tyra's pull, as she prayed for him to turn his head in her direction. But, he made her wait until praise and worship began. When he finally looked over at Tyra, her appearance caught him off guard.

Man oh man; she's even lovelier when she works at it!

He smiled, mouthing the words, "Good morning, Tyra."

She mouthed an adoring, "Hello, Wilson."

Tyra thought she felt her heart skip a beat.

When the service ended, Tyra tried not to panic as she saw Wilson slip out. The favorable reactions to her new look caused her to be held up by several hugs and compliments. Tyra thanked each admirer, trying not to seem rude as she hurried to the door.

She was relieved and overjoyed to see Wilson waiting for her, at the bus stop.

"Hi, Wilson, so you came. How did you enjoy the service?"

"Hello there, lady. The service was great. I will definitely be back."

"Oh, that's wonderful. So maybe your prayer for a church home has been answered?"

Tyra immediately regretted her words. *I'm being too pushy*, she thought.

Wilson caught the eagerness in her tone, but he decided to change the subject.

"Tyra, may I say that you look lovely? You are the epitome of inner and outer beauty."

"Thank you, Wilson. You're so kind."

"You're quite welcome."

At that point, Wilson took Tyra's arm and gently began leading her down the street, toward his car.

"Tyra, I usually keep my car parked during the week, but I'm driving today. It would be my pleasure to chauffer you anywhere you'd like to go. As a matter of fact, do you have plans for dinner?"

"Well, I was invited to my cousin's house, but I didn't give her a definite answer."

"Does that I mean I might convince you to have dinner with me?"

"Why, yes, I can be convinced," Tyra answered from a sincere heart.

"Well, I'd consider it an honor and a privilege to take you to dinner."

Wilson unlocked his Lexus and opened the passenger door. Tyra's journey into night had begun.

Wilson pulled out all the stops for their first date. He'd already reserved a table at his favorite restaurant. There was never a doubt in his mind that she'd join him for dinner. It was still early when they reached Manhattan, so Wilson suggested a stroll in Central Park. He bought Tyra flowers and made a point to smile warmly at all the little children they saw.

Opal's Supper Club was like something out of a vintage movie. Intimate tables clothed in white linen flanked a live jazz ensemble, in a half-moon layout. A small dance floor filled the center space. It was obvious that Wilson was a regular.

"Welcome, Mr. Yearwood, it's my pleasure to seat you this evening."

"Thank you, Sidney. We'll just need a minute."

"Yes, of course, I'm at your service."

Sidney presented them with menus and stepped away on cue. Wilson smiled warmly, as he reached across the table with his eyes. Tyra smiled back, falling deeper into his web.

"Tyra, please have whatever you like. The chef does wonders with everything."

"Oh my, let's see. The sea bass sounds delicious. But, so does the rib eye. Wilson, I can't decide."

"I understand. Shall I choose for you?"

"Oh yes, Wilson. I trust your judgment."

It was a delightful meal. The entree included an opulent medley of surf and turf. From the appetizers to the dessert, each course was absolute perfection.

The conversation over dinner went according to Wilson's agenda. As Tyra poured her heart out, Wilson gained the information needed to customize his words. He'd start by applauding her career choice.

"I'm not at all surprised that you're in pediatric medicine. It takes a very special person to balance compassion with professionalism and get the job done. A lot of people would lose it, at the sight of a desperately ill child. I know I would."

"God gives me grace for it. And you're so right about the need for balance.

But you could not have understood that without your own degree of insight and sensitivity. I think there's a lot more to you than meets the eye, Mr. Yearwood. I noticed your reaction to the children in the park."

"Well, Tyra, you busted me. Yes, I do have a tender streak. But don't hold it against me, okay?"

He's a sweetheart, she thought. *Thank you Lord.*

"Wilson, your secret is safe with me. Be as tender as you'd like."

Then Wilson's Colgate smile faded. He replaced it with a well-honed expression of vulnerability that melted Tyra's heart.

"I'm going to hold you to that," Wilson replied. He reached across the table and squeezed her hand. Tyra squeezed back.

For the rest of the evening, Wilson spoke words to seduce the soul of a lonely 30-year-old misfit, still mourning the loss of her parents. His compliments affirmed the book worm that almost never got asked to parties. He declared her beauty and her worthiness of the love she so desperately longed for.

Most of all, Wilson planted the false hope of a future that would never be – not with him. Tyra was so gullible. Wilson just couldn't resist his mack daddy play. These lines were usually reserved for subsequent dates.

"Tyra, I don't care if traditional values are not politically correct. For me, marriage is still an honorable institution. If I'm ever blessed to walk down that aisle, it will be for keeps. Although some would disagree, I believe that the husband has a duty to make it work, when the going gets rough. The groom lays down his life for his bride, not the other way around!"

If Tyra had been standing, she would have gone weak in the knees.

"I feel blessed to know you, Wilson. I've never had such a wonderful time."

"Tyra, I feel the same. Shall we head back to Crown Heights?"

"Okay, Wilson."

As they walked hand in hand to his car, Tyra wanted to pinch herself.

Although it was still early when they arrived back in Brooklyn, Wilson declined Tyra's invitation to come inside.

"We both have work tomorrow. Besides, I don't want to wear out my welcome on the first date. Tyra, I surely hope this is just the first of many dates."

"I hope so too, Wilson."

"I'm glad to hear that. So, maybe we should exchange numbers?"

"Oh gosh, Wilson, we never did that, did we?"

The two laughed as they reached for their iPhones. Wilson walked her to the door. There, he kissed Tyra's hand and returned to his car.

The evening was a complete success for Wilson. He'd gained an intimate profile on Tyra while sharing very little of himself.

Tyra learned that he grew up in Fort Greene. After graduating from N.Y.U., he cut his teeth in the New York City Comptroller's Office. Five years ago, he started his own accounting firm. Wilson owned two rental properties in North Carolina, and he recently purchased an apartment in Flatbush. Almost nothing was revealed that couldn't be obtained from a business bio.

But, that didn't matter to Tyra. After one date, she believed that she loved Wilson. And she wanted him more than anything. Maestro Wilson had crafted his every expression to pull at Tyra's heart strings. And, the music created would be to his delight.

Several agonizing days would follow as the love-sick Tyra waited for Wilson to call. Somehow, she resisted the urge to make the first move.

I just can't call him. It would be too forward. Lord, please let him call me.

It was almost a week before Wilson picked up the phone. As he intended, Tyra was overjoyed to hear his voice.

"Hello Tyra, how are you sweetheart?"

"I'm fine, Wilson, how are you?"

"I'm tired but thankful to be back in town. One of my properties in Fayetteville was vandalized by a dispossessed tenant. I just touched down at LaGuardia."

"Oh, I'm so sorry to hear that."

"As a landlord, it goes with the territory."

"I'm just glad you're okay. I missed you...I hope I don't sound too forward."

"Not at all, in fact those words are music to my ears. Tyra, I missed you too. Let's see, today is Friday. Do you have plans for Saturday?"

"No, I don't have plans. Wilson, I was thinking about cooking for you. How would you like a home cooked meal?"

"Oh, that would be such a blessing. Are you sure it's not too much trouble?"

"It's no trouble at all. I'd love to share my table with you. What do you like to eat?"

"Baby, I eat almost anything except meatloaf."

"No problem, how about veal piccata?"

"I'd love it. What time?"

"Let's say 6:00 pm?"

"I'll be there. Thank you so much, Tyra. This means more to me than you know."

"You're so welcome, take care, Wilson."

"You do the same, sweetheart."

"Alright, that was easy," Wilson grinned, as he hung up the phone, turned over, and went to sleep.

It was widely known by friends and family that cooking was Tyra's love language. Now, at last, there was someone special to cook for. She was beside herself.

A good man deserves the blessing of a good meal. And I'm going to cook a meal to bless his socks off!

The next day, Wilson rang her door bell at 6:00 pm, sharp. He arrived with chilled champagne, roses, and a gift set of Mademoiselle by Chanel.

"Thank you, Wilson, I don't know what to say. You're going to spoil me."

"Tyra, you deserve so much more. May I help you with anything?"

"Would you please open the wine, I'm no good at cork screws. I'll just grab a vase for the flowers."

Wilson filled the crystal wine flutes, as Tyra plated their meal. What she brought to the table was a feast for the eyes, and the appetite. The platter of tender veal and pasta was seasoned with just the right amount of lemon, capers and garlic. Then she ended the meal with homemade ricotta cheese cake and freshly ground espressos.

"Thank you, Tyra. This was a delicious taste of Little Italy. I'm very impressed."

"You're so welcome. Cooking brings me joy, and I love all kinds of cuisine. I can take you around the world, from my kitchen, if you'd like."

"Oh, I'd like that very much."

"You're on, Mr. Yearwood." They tapped glasses, to seal the deal.

Wilson and Tyra made an attractive couple, as they enjoyed each other in her lovely place. Tyra looked stunning, in a turquoise empire waist tunic dress. Wilson was equally sharp, in charcoal gabardine slacks and a button collar shirt, minus the tie.

On the surface it appeared innocent enough. However, candlelight, wine, and music have a way of softening edges, and relaxing safeguards.

It wasn't clear how they moved from the dining table to her sofa. But, somewhere between the end of dessert and the goodbye kiss, Tyra had been changed. His touch had forever ended her ignorance of sensual pleasure.

Right afterwards, she'd pushed him away, embarrassed and shaken, by what he'd caused her to feel.

"Wilson, I'm a virgin. I want to keep myself for my husband. I'm sorry if I misled you – I didn't mean to lead you on."

Kowabunga, thought Wilson – *a virgin!*

Of course, his outward response to her was much more sensitive. "Tyra, I understand, and I have the utmost respect for you. Please forgive me for getting carried away. My heart got away from my head."

"I'm sorry too. Wilson, let's agree to have no more wine and smooth jazz when we're alone, okay?"

"Okay, sweetheart."

But, Wilson knew very well what he'd awakened in Tyra. From then on, there'd be no need for wine and music.

After he left, Tyra opened Wilson's gift and ran a bubble bath. The luxurious fragrance filled the room but did nothing to soothe her soul. She was fearful and didn't know why.

Why am I so upset? Nothing has happened.

Tyra failed to pray that night. Before sleep came, she'd uttered another kind of plea.

"Oh, Wilson, I hope you are the one. Please be the one."

As time passed, Tyra began to see her lack of intimate experience as a handicap, instead of the blessing that it was. She'd always believed that sexual intimacy was reserved for marriage. Now, another voice had surfaced, to mock the beliefs that had kept her for years.

Tyra was clueless regarding the seed that had been planted in her soul, with crafted words, and a handshake. But nevertheless, that seed was bearing fruit.

Her desire for Wilson led her to ignore the still, small voice. Tyra was looking for approval, not truth.

She meditated on the motto of her church: *Living Word Fellowship is a Refuge for the 21st Century Believer.*

Grasping at straws, Tyra reasoned that maybe those Scripture verses about fornication are not for today. *If they were still relevant, wouldn't my pastor be teaching them?*

In her time of need, Tyra had no sermonic CD to play. There were no study notes to combat the encroaching danger. The message at Living Word fell short of Biblical teaching.

Single women were instructed not to give themselves to men, who had no intentions of marriage. And promiscuous behavior was strongly denounced.

But, Pastor Bush had never preached a sermon against fornication. After all, that kind of teaching might offend his congregation, which could result in a decrease in offerings and membership. In order to grow, Living Word Fellowship had to be run like any other business. He didn't need a leadership conference to figure that out.

And so, all things considered, Wilson was bound to succeed in his quest for Tyra. He cruised through the bases, virtually unopposed. In just a matter of weeks, her pearl would be cast before swine.

After it happened, Tyra was led to believe that there was no turning back for her. She gave audience to the enemy, who convinced her that marriage to Wilson was her only hope. If they became man and wife, that would cleanse her of the nagging guilt and affirm her choice.

It would also validate Wilson's proclamations of love, not only for her, but for her family's benefit as well. She just needed to hang in there. Wilson would marry her, once she assured him of her love and faithfulness.

Over the months that followed, Tyra began to distance herself from Abby. Except for her spa appointments, the two rarely saw one another.

But they'd always been close and Abby was able to discern that Tyra was in trouble. She would not stand by and let her home girl be destroyed. After several declines, Tyra finally agreed to meet her for a girl's night-in.

After they dined on some delicious take-out from RenewVation's gourmet bistro, Abby made an attempt to reach out to her best friend.

"So how are things with you and Wilson?"

At first Tyra began singing Wilson's praises. But the sadness in her voice revealed the burden she carried in her heart.

"Nothing's changed Abby, we're still in love. I believe that he'll make it official sometime soon."

Abby's pained expression put Tyra on the defensive.

"Abby, this is my life, okay. I'm sorry you don't approve."

"Oh Ty, can't you see what's happening? It's been almost a year and all he does is dodge the issue of marriage. You're good enough to sleep with, make his meals, and clean his house, but he won't even be seen with you, except around strangers! He disappears and reappears, without notice. Baby, you deserve better than this."

"Abby, you don't understand. He just needs some time. Marriage is a big commitment for some men."

"Ty, what about your commitment, the commitment you made to God? Have you forgotten the vow of purity that we took?"

"Abby, that feels like a million years ago. I'm at the point of no return here. If Wilson is not the one, then that means I gave myself to him in vain. No, I just need to stand on faith that he will come around."

"Come around, you say? He won't even come around your family. Why is that?"

"I think he feels that you won't like him."

"Ty, why would he think that if his intentions were right? Why won't he sit with you in church, or even acknowledge to anyone there that he knows you?"

"I should never have mentioned that to you. Abby, he's thinking of my reputation in the church."

"Oh, I see. How thoughtful of him. And speaking of church, I caught Pastor Bush on the radio one morning. Living Word Fellowship has some strange ideas about standing on faith."

"Don't go there, Cuz. Living Word spoke to my needs the minute I joined."

"No, Ty, it spoke to your desires. And how's that working for you, now? Ty, the devil can speak also. He masquerades as an angel of light.

Faith is not about the acquisition of things or people. Our faith is in God. And another thing, you are not at the point of no return. There is grace for you to turn around."

By this time, both women were losing their battle to keep from crying.

"Listen Abby, I came over because you said that you missed me. I've missed you too. But, I can't deal with this right now. I'm no longer where you are, but don't condemn me for it. I have to get home now. Give everyone my love."

Before Abby could respond, Tyra hugged her neck and rushed out the door. It was a painful departure for both of them.

Later that evening, Abby called Josh to talk about the failed intervention. It would be an eye-opening experience.

"Abby, you are our father's daughter."

"And what does that mean?"

"Dad loves to fix things, and he's good at it. But, sometimes he tries to fix people and that never works. Abby, you can save a bad hair day and correct a fashion mistake, like nobody else. But, that's all on the surface. Only God can fix the inside."

"Josh, this is our girl, how can I stand by and do nothing?"

"I didn't say that you should do nothing."

"Well, what do you suggest?"

"I suggest prayer and supplication. Ty's soul is tied to this dude. She needs to be restored gently. And Sis, you need to remember that she has not sinned against you."

"Come again?"

"Okay, when we sin, we sin against *God*."

"I know that, Josh."

"Yeah, but sometimes it's easy to forget what we know when those we love fall short. If not for His grace, you may have broken *your* vow of purity."

Right then her brother's words struck a chord. Abby felt the conviction of God.

"Thank you, Jesus!"

"Josh, I'm so glad I called you. I'm afraid I acted without His leading. I don't know what God is doing, but Ty belongs to Him, and no demon in hell can change that. I think we need to intercede for her."

"Absolutely, let's stand in agreement here and now."

After they prayed, Abby was led to fast, for understanding and direction.

A month went by. It had been days since Tyra had seen Wilson, and he was not returning her calls. His pattern of disappearances had begun to eat away at her self-respect, causing Tyra to become more and more insecure.

She had never gone to his house uninvited. Tonight would be a first. As the taxi sped Tyra toward her appointment with destiny, she rehearsed her position, over and over in her mind.

I've been patient regarding his need for time, but my needs are not being met. This is not the life I want. This is not what God wants for me. Surely Wilson can see that, if he really loves me.

Tyra had given Wilson a key to her home, but he'd never gotten around to returning the gesture. She was relieved to see his Lexus parked in front of the building. Still, her heart raced as she approached his door and rang the bell. There was soft music coming from inside. Why wasn't he answering the door?

Oh my God, she thought, *I hope he's alright.* Tyra dialed his number again but it went straight to voice mail.

Then, all of a sudden, the mystery was solved. Wilson's muted words were not clearly heard by Tyra. But the woman's voice was loud and clear.

"Don't tell me to be quiet. And no, I'm not going to disappear anywhere."

The muffled sounds continued. Then Tyra heard the voice again.
"I don't care who she is. This is our time!"

Tyra wanted to scream but she was stunned speechless. She turned from Wilson's door, and found herself back out on the street. As she wandered aimlessly, too hurt to cry, a mix of conflicting emotions consumed her.

How do I react to this? I want to kill him. No, I want to hold him close.

After walking a few blocks, Tyra looked up at the street sign and found herself on Nostrand Avenue. The smell of curry and jerk drew her into a Jamaican café. Ignoring the waitress who offered to seat her, Tyra stared blankly at the chalk board menu, wondering when she had eaten last.

What does food matter when my world is falling apart? She walked out and continued her trek.

At some point the neighborhood changed. Tyra drifted through a crowd of men with eyes full of ganja and smiles filled with mischief. She was on another high, one born of grief, far removed from any sense of her surroundings.

By the time she reached Herkimer Street Tyra was ready to collapse. Overcome by nausea, she turned in to an alley where she lost her only meal of the day. Leaning back against the wall, she cried out to the Lord.

Oh God, It hurts so much. I don't know what to do. Jesus, please help me.

In time, her panic began to subside. Sweet music filled her ears and she was drawn across the street to a storefront church.

It was revival week at House of Grace. An elderly woman greeted her warmly as she entered.

"Welcome, daughter, thank you for coming."

The woman exuded a love that only comes from time spent with Jesus. Tyra wanted to fall into her arms and hug her neck.

"I'm glad to be here, mother."

As the psalmist sang "Speak to My Heart" Tyra sat with her head bowed. She felt herself yielding to a sweet surrender. It brought to mind the day she received her prayer language.

Lord, I've missed our time together. I want to feel clean again.

When the praise team stepped down, Pastor Roderick Sherman gave the altar call that would change her life.

"Some of you have found yourselves in a dry place as the cares of this world distracted you. You may have even turned away, deceived by the lusts of the flesh."

Tyra groaned softly as she heard the pastor continue.

"But, God wants you to know that you have not been utterly cast down. He's been keeping you through the sifting process. Beloved, your faith has not failed. That's why you're here. The arms of Jesus are open to receive you. Won't you come?"

Tyra was the first person in line. Tears of repentance fell freely, as she made her way to the front. The presence of God was so heavy; she could hardly stand upright. When she approached the pastor, he spoke softly in her ear, as the Spirit led.

"My sister, I see two wombs: one in grave danger and one destined to bring forth lasting fruit. You will leave this place with a desire for God that surpasses that which has had you bound. Grace will enable you to resist the enemy. And you will answer God's call to holiness, as the love of Abba Father consumes you."

Then the man of God laid hands on Tyra, and she went down. She felt herself in motion for a time. When she came to a rest, someone gently helped her onto a chair.

After the service, a young lady from the praise team drove her home.

"May I see you inside, Sister Tyra?"

"No thanks, Alice. I'll be fine from here."

"Okay, we'll be praying for you."

"Thanks so much."

Alice waited for Tyra to enter her building, before driving away. When she stepped off the elevator, Wilson was waiting at her door. He looked like he wanted to cry.

"Hello Tyra. Baby, it's so late. I was beginning to worry. I was so upset I somehow misplaced my key."

Tyra did not reply. She unlocked the door and stepped inside. Wilson followed her in. As he began to sob all over her foyer, Tyra saw through him, for the first time.

"Wilson, if you don't leave, I will have to call for assistance."

"Tyra please, let me explain. She means nothing to me. It was a moment of weakness that will never happen again. I want to spend my life with you."

"Wilson, God has revealed something different to me. He has destroyed the yoke. I'm free, do you hear? As of tomorrow, your key will no longer fit. I'm afraid you have to leave, now."

Wilson calmed himself and dried his eyes. "Okay Tyra, I'll leave, but I won't give up on us. I love you too much."

The Father's affirmation was palpable, as Tyra closed the door behind Wilson. She dropped to her knees in the living room. Worship came forth, from a broken and contrite heart. The love of God overwhelmed her. Tyra remained prostrate for a time, just basking in the glory.

But her mountain top experience would end with an abrupt descent into the valley. As Tyra tried to stand, her body began to convulse with a pain that was unbearable. She flashed hot and cold all over, as the room started to spin out of focus. Then, Tyra's body went into free-fall.

At that very moment, a few blocks away, Abby was awakened by an Inner voice. *Tyra needs you. Go to her*.

Abby had no doubt regarding the Messenger. She was out of bed and into a jogging suit in minutes. On her way out the door, she called Josh.

"Tyra's in trouble, meet me at her house. And, please call Mom and Dad. Ask them to intercede."

Fortunately, the cousins had exchanged house keys, as each

of them became homeowners. Abby rang the doorbell and immediately entered with her key.

She found Tyra on the living room floor and dialed 911. Help was dispatched, as Abby felt for signs of life and continued to pray.

"Abba Father, have mercy in Jesus' name. Ty, please hold on." As she continued in prayer, Tyra started to moan.

"Wilson never loved me. He never did."

"It's alright baby, everything's okay."

"I had to end it all. But Jesus still loves me."

"Tyra, what do you mean? Ty, please talk to me, open your eyes!"

Just then, Josh rushed in. "Sis, what happened?"

"I don't know."

"Pills?"

"I don't know!"

Tyra was unresponsive by the time the paramedics arrived. Abby dialed her parents again, who were already en route from Queens. She redirected them to the hospital.

It was an hour before Dr. Colin Greene, the physician on call appeared in the waiting room. Dr. Greene informed the family that Tyra had suffered a ruptured, tubal pregnancy. No, it was not an overdose of pills that caused her to collapse.

Once that was settled, the doctor gently began a barrage of verbiage used so often in medical dramas. *"It is a miracle that she survived. She's not out of the woods yet. The next hours are critical..."*

The Redding family listened politely to the one that practiced medicine. But, their hope rested in the One that held Tyra's life in His hands. From the hospital chapel, throughout the night, prayers went up on Tyra's behalf.

Wilson spent a sleepless night, as well. After hours of tossing and turning, he rose from the bed and sought to encourage himself. But, as he gazed into the mirror, something was wrong. The facade had been lifted. A lost soul, in all of its depravity, stared back at him.

It was too much to bear. With a loud cry, Wilson grabbed a bottle from his dresser, and hurled it at his BFF. Brute after shave filled the air, as he proclaimed to his shattered image, "No woman walks away from me. We can't let her get away!"

When morning came, a determined Wilson set out for the New York City Jewelry Exchange. As he entered one of the stores, Wilson's corporate attire made it clear that he was ready, and able, to do business.

"May I help you, Sir?"

"Yes, I'm interested in a diamond engagement ring. Show me what you have in a one carat round cut, surrounded by sapphires, set in white gold."

As the jeweler, led him over to the diamond cases, Wilson muttered under his breath, "I won't lose Tyra. She'll get her ring. But a ring doesn't have to mean marriage."

"Excuse me, Sir?"

"Oh, nothing," Wilson smiled. "I was just talking to myself. Listen, my fiancée is really special and I want something that is worthy of her."

"Well, Sir, you have come to the right place. If you don't see it here, we can create it for you."

"That's what I want to hear. So, let's have a look."

Wilson left the store that day having purchased the ring he believed would lure Tyra back. It never occurred to him that she had been serious about the breakup.

After three days of trying to reach her by phone, Wilson arrived at Tyra's condo, having found the lost key. Abby and Josh were there. Tyra had sent them to change the lock, collect the mail, and pick up some things for her.

"What? I can't believe she changed the lock on me!"

Wilson rang the bell. Josh opened the door. Introductions were made in Tyra's foyer. The encounter was less than cordial.

"So, where's my baby? We had a little lovers' quarrel, and I see she changed the locks on me."

Abby, at a loss for acceptable words, was doing her best to keep silent. Josh was curt and to the point.

"Wilson, our cousin has been in the ICU at Kings County for the past three days."

"Wow, the ICU? Come to think of it, she wasn't looking too well lately. I knew something must be wrong. It's not like my baby to ignore my calls. Well, I hope you know that I intend to be there for her."

The two siblings exchanged glances, making no effort to hide their disgust. Then Josh turned back to Wilson and dismissed him with a warning.

"Wilson, we need to get back to the hospital, to relieve our parents. I hope you know that the ICU is restricted to the immediate family."

"Of course, I understand. Hopefully, it won't be long before I can see her. We have importance things to discuss."

Abby broke her silence.

"Listen, Wilson, Ty has moved on. She made that fact clear to me when I found her near death."

"Well, I'm sure she didn't realize what she was saying. Listen, please tell Tyra that I'll see her as soon as I'm able and give her my love."

"You really need to leave. Josh, tell him."

Josh voiced his agreement. "Wilson, I think you better leave, now."

And so, Wilson departed, leaving the two siblings trying to clear their heads.

"Abby, he never even asked what happened to her!"

"I know. Ty has been to hell and back."

A few days later Wilson showed up at Kings County Medical. He approached the nursing station minutes before visiting hours were over. With a dozen long stemmed roses and his Colgate smile, he checked the name tag of the most timid looking staff member.

"Hello, Ms. Chang, I'm here to see Ms. Tyra Redding. I understand she was just moved to this floor from the ICU."

The ward clerk's demeanor was polite but guarded. "If you'd hold on a second, I'll get the nurse."

"Why do you need to get the nurse? Please tell Ms. Redding that Wilson Yearwood is here. I'm sure she wants to see me. I'm her fiancé."

"I'll be right back, Mr. Yearwood."

After a brief exchange and a phone call to Tyra's room, the head nurse appeared, looking anything but timid.

"Hello, Mr. Yearwood. I'm Lisa Rowland, the head nurse. Ms. Redding's condition has been upgraded to stable. However, she has requested that no visitors be admitted except for the immediate family."

By that time Wilson was seething with anger but his smile remained intact.

"There must be some mistake. Please let her know that I'm here."

"Mr. Yearwood, I informed Ms. Redding of your presence and I passed on the message you gave Ms. Chang."

"And what did she say?"

"She informed me that she has no fiancé. Perhaps you'd like to speak with a family member? Her cousins are with her. They have offered to speak with you."

At that point the frozen smile cracked. Wilson uttered his reply through clenched teeth.

"No thank you, Ms. Rowland, I don't care to speak with her cousins." Wilson had no desire to repeat that experience.

After an unsuccessful attempt to stare the head nurse down, he turned and stalked away.

"Mr. Yearwood, you're forgetting your flowers…well, have a good evening!"

Ms. Rowland barely contained her amusement as the angry little man stormed out into the elevator court.

Back at home, Wilson was confronted with his broken mirror. Its shattered image taunted him from across the room as he paced the floor.

"You're trying to mock me? Well, I have something for you!"

He covered the mirror with a sheet and sat down on the bed to gather his thoughts.

Tyra must be suffering from some post traumatic confusion. And those cousins of hers aren't blameless either; they turned her against me. Nothing can ruin a good relationship like meddling relations!

But I just need to regroup and remain steadfast. She'll come to her senses as soon as she's well again. We'll get back on track. All I need is the opportunity to stage the moment. I mean, how can I fail with diamonds and sapphires?

Tyra left the hospital that next week and was pampered through her recuperation at Abby's house. When she returned to the condo, Wilson resumed his campaign to win her back. Her mailbox overflowed with cards and letters. She waded through flowers and candles left at her front door.

But Tyra gave him no encouragement. All of his gifts went in the trash. She even changed her phone number and e-mail address.

Eventually, Tyra returned to work. But, as time passed she showed no signs of wanting to resume her position as Wilson's main squeeze. All of Wilson's gestures were failing and his patience was wearing thin. It was time for a more direct approach.

He knew that Tyra worked a double every other Friday. There in the main lobby of Children's Hospital, Wilson decided to stage his most dramatic effort to win her back. He arrived one Saturday morning at the end of her last shift.

As Tyra stepped off the elevator and headed for the exit, Wilson rose to intercept her path.

"Wilson, why are you here? I'm sorry but there's nothing more to be said. "

"Hello, Tyra. Can I just have a minute, please?"

Seeing Wilson now, she couldn't believe that she had ever wanted to marry the man.

How could I have been so blind?

Tyra reluctantly took a seat. "You have one minute, Wilson."

But Wilson mistook pity for weakness and was emboldened. He sat down beside her.

"Tyra, I'm so sorry that you were hurt. I understand now that you don't want the kind of relationship we had before. But if you'd give me another chance, I'd like to make it up to you."

Wilson did not wait for a reply. Going down on one knee he reached into his suit jacket and pulled out the spectacular engagement ring. "Will you marry me, Tyra, and accept this symbol of my loving affection?"

There was no hesitation in Tyra's reply. "No, Wilson, I will not. Now, if you'll excuse me, I really have to be going."

Wilson stared in disbelief as Tyra stood and walked away. When she disappeared from view he rose to his feet. Making a prideful exit from the lobby, he went home to lick his wounds.

Once again, he sought refuge in self-pity.

"I offered her diamonds and sapphires, and she threw them back in my face!"

In bitter resignation the numbers man fingered his costly purchase and was glad to have kept the receipt. He comforted himself with a vow to even the score.

"I guess nice guys do finish last. Well, there's more where she came from and next time there will be no Mr. Nice Guy!"

Meanwhile, God continued to honor those prayers that went up on Tyra's behalf. They were in keeping with His will. Her restoration was full and purposeful.

She started attending House of Grace where the ministers labored to make disciples, by the Spirit.

But, her new church home would be more than a place of worship. In time it became the training ground for Tyra's call to strengthen the brethren. Having received God's comfort, the gifted nurturer would be used to minister that same comfort to others.

Pastor Sherman took note of the chosen vessel whose testimony would edify so many in their call to live for Christ.

He saw in her a precious treasure and committed all things to Jesus. God is so good.

Amen.

Not by Works

"For it is by grace you have been saved, through faith - and this is not from yourselves, it is the gift of God - not by works, so that no one can boast."
~Ephesians 2:8-9

Not by Works

Nola Daniel's journey of self-acceptance had come full circle. In the 57th year of her life, she gazed into the mirror and received her image with gladness.

She had no desire to turn the clock back twenty years. Nor was there the fear of what image the next twenty years might reveal. In this respect, Nola could laugh at the days to come.

As she whispered a "Thank you, Father," there came a knock on her bedroom door.

"How're you doing, my sister, are you ready for your comb-out?"

"Yes, thanks, come on in."

Jean Redding entered the room and smiled at her very best friend since elementary school. At first, no words came forth. But, the silent conversation spoke volumes, and a mutual flow of tears threatened to ruin the professional makeup applied just minutes ago.

"I guess we should have used the water-proof mascara,"

Jean fussed as she gingerly wiped her friend's eyes with the last Kleenex in the box. She then, absentmindedly, began to wipe her own eyes with the same soggy tissue. Nola smiled at the sight.

"Jean, do you remember the last time we shared a snot rag?"

"Uh hum, it was at St. Patrick's Cathedral when they killed Robert Kennedy."

"That's right. After school, we joined the stream of dazed mourners. In one turbulent decade, we lost Kennedy, Medgar, Malcolm, King, and then Kennedy, again."

For a brief moment they reflected on the times and events that shaped their lives and changed the nation.

Suddenly, Nola started pacing back and forth like she was ready to preach.

"But you know Jean, through it all, God kept us."

Jean nodded in agreement and glanced at her watch.

Lord there's no time to redo her make-up again. Please let her keep it together. Jean kept praying silently as the bride continued to testify.

"And for me, this day of His keeping will mark the realization of a very personal milestone. Just imagine, in a little less than one hour this battle-scarred veteran of unsanctified relationships will become a wife, and my God is well pleased!"

"Yes, He is, my sister, but first, we've got to get you ready. So please come on over here and sit down."

Nola took a seat at the dressing table, and Jean began removing her hair rollers.

Those closest to the author and Bible teacher understood that the union about to take place had been divinely orchestrated. They had seen the Lord move mightily so many times in Nola's life.

Six years ago Nola left her nine-to-five and found provision through the ministry gift of teaching. Leaving the reliable comfort of a scheduled paycheck for a walk of faith had been both liberating and frightening. But, the undeniable urging of the Spirit and His assurance that her time had come to move was all she had needed.

Nola committed herself to be about the Lord's business, and never looked back. God was faithful and her service bore fruit. Individuals who had never entered a church building were receiving salvation and discipleship at her workshops and Bible studies for small groups. Her books were well received by believers as tools of edification.

Resisting the urge to bemoan the time it had taken to reach this point, she believed that her years were not wasted, and the best was yet to come.

And, so, as Jean styled her hair into a vintage-inspired bouffant, Nola's thoughts were focused on the wedding vows that would be taken … and consummated that evening. No one could have seen this day coming except through the eyes of faith.

Nola had been married before. It had been an abusive relationship, bent on her destruction. But, Jesus silenced the enemy and had the final say.

After the divorce, she began to yield to the Father's love and was ushered into a new level of intimacy with Him. She gained considerable insight into that mystery regarding Christ and His church and harbored no bitterness. Doors were opened for her to share what she'd received with the brethren.

Because wisdom had taught her to never, say never, Nola had remained open to the possibility of remarriage, provided it would better serve God's purpose for her. However, the general consensus was that she'd finish her race as one devoted exclusively to the Lord's affairs.

Graced to walk in celibacy for more than a decade and at peace with the idea of remaining so, Nola had been a role model for the unmarried women of God who crossed her path.

Now, as she stepped into a fitted blush colored sheath with lace overlay, Nola considered how her life was about to change. She couldn't help but think back and marvel at the Lord's mysterious ways.

It was two years ago that something remarkable started to happen. What began as subtle nuances, easily dismissed, were suddenly invading Nola's thoughts at the most inopportune times.

In the midst of the homiletics and hermeneutics, she began to imagine herself ...married!

Her first response was denial. She voiced her rebuttals out loud.

"I'm not honoring this mess with my time, it's not even real."

As the thoughts prevailed, she moved to the rebuking, defensive mode.

"If I resist, surely they will flee."

Nola reasoned that God had given her the gift of singleness and her job was to defend it. After weeks of struggling alone, with no relief, she declared that this was all out spiritual warfare and decided to call for back-up.

She phoned Jean and invited her to dinner (no need to alarm her with any details upfront).

Actually, Nola was feeling a little embarrassed about the whole thing. Nevertheless, she was determined and confident that in the end her BFF and prayer partner would touch and agree with her for victory over this attack.

Somehow, Nola failed to realize that her steadfast warfare was causing her to neglect worship. This rendered her unprepared for the response of her tried and true friend.

Jean accepted the dinner invitation with enthusiasm. Nola's cooking *made your tongue slap your brains out!* And that would be a welcome change from the catered meals she'd been sharing recently with her husband, Will. Even gourmet take-out was still take-out.

After 35 years of marriage, Jean and her hubby were enjoying their empty nest in Cambria Heights. Their two children, Josh and Abigail, had moved out and purchased homes of their own.

In defiance of the stats and stereotypes, the two siblings were responsible and productive, building on the foundation of hard work and community service laid by their parents.

Abby had transformed the marketing of Pure Grace, her mother's natural cosmetics line, from a single kiosk to a thriving online enterprise. Pure Grace was also the exclusive skincare available at RenewVation, the family-owned day spas, meticulously managed by Josh and Abby.

The first spa, which opened just five years ago, had multiplied into three very busy locations in Brooklyn, Queens, and Manhattan. Last year, a gourmet bistro was added to the flagship spa on Fulton Street.

Will and Jean still attended quarterly meetings and provided valuable input regarding RenewVation's mission to nurture the body and soul of each guest. However, the day-to-day operations of the business were now in the capable hands of their son and daughter.

At last, Mr. and Mrs. Redding were free to enjoy both individual and collective rediscovery. Most weeknights the kitchen was closed and no one was mad. Neither one cared to venture into whether this was a temporary phase or a permanent arrangement. Knowing what worked for them without violating God's word had kept them thus far.

And so, on the evening of her dinner invitation, Jean kissed her husband good-bye, handed him the remote and promised to bring home a plate, as their friend always made more than enough for leftovers.

Nola was in the kitchen, putting the finishing touches on a succulent meal of pan broiled salmon with lemon-caper white wine sauce, angel hair pasta with sun dried tomatoes, and sautéed artichoke hearts. A sweet potato pie was cooling on the buffet.

Nola's home was a peaceful refuge from the manifold insanities of the world. The renovated Bed-Stuy brownstone provided a warm and inviting place for friends to take their shoes off and enjoy the gift of hospitality.

Having been banned from the kitchen by her hostess, Jean curled up on the butter soft leather sofa, sipping mint tea. "Holy is the Lamb" played softly in the background. The warm glow of the fireplace had a soothing effect.

It crossed Jean's mind that the purpose of tonight's invitation might be more than fellowship and good food. But, she pulled the chenille throw up around her and decided not to press her friend. Nola would open up if and when she was ready, not before. Just as the aromas began to taunt Jean's hunger, Nola announced dinner.

Conversation was kept light during the meal. Nola stalled, requesting make-up tips, and Jean played along, requesting recipes. Neither of them had the slightest intention of using the information they'd received and that was just fine.

The dishes were in the washer and Will's plate was in the fridge when Nola blurted out, "I think I'm losing my gift."

Jean stared at her for a few seconds before replying, "Okay... what gift?"

"You know," said Nola, *the* gift!

Another blank stare ensued.

"Okay, how about I name a gift and you tell me if I've guessed the gift that you think you're losing."

"This is not funny, Jean."

"Do you see me laughing, Nola? You're the one who has turned this into a guessing game."

Jean leaned against the dishwasher, facing her friend, while trying unsuccessfully to look serious. Nola turned away and began wiping the spotless range top like her life depended on it.

Jean continued her playful banter.

"So, what gift do you think you're losing? It can't be the teaching gift. Not by Works Ministries continues to be a blessing to the church. Surely it's not the gift of hospitality because right now, I'm as well-fed and pampered as always. Nola, I'm convinced that you are your worst critic. You need to lighten up!"

"It's the gift of singleness, Jean. I'm afraid I'm losing the gift of singleness."

Nola had this way of smiling through tears when things were really bad. She turned to Jean with eyes that were about to spill over, despite the dimpled half grin. Her expression revealed a place of fear, seldom visited and very rarely shared.

Jean embraced her friend and prayed silently for wisdom as they walked into the living room.

Two cozy side chairs flanked the hand carved coffee table. They sat down facing one another. Jean spoke first.

"I'm so sorry, Nola. You seemed a little distracted lately but I thought it was your hectic schedule. I was actually going to suggest a Caribbean vacation intervention. And, please forgive me for not hearing your heart just now. I didn't mean to be insensitive."

"Apology accepted," Nola replied, drying her eyes with the back of her hand.

"You know even as God uses me to instruct others, I'm also a disciple working out my salvation with fear and trembling. Jean, sometimes I feel that I have no right to confess to being less than what everybody expects.

But, I need to be able to talk to someone. You knew me years before I fell on the altar and confessed Jesus as Lord."

"Nola, I've seen how you turn-off when people try to put you on a pedestal. Please believe that you can be open with me."

Jean then asked a question. "Are your feelings the result of thoughts, words, or actions?"

"That's a good question. I'm having these thoughts. I've begun to imagine myself married and content. I mean really content – do you know what I mean?"

"Uh hum girl, I know," Jean replied.

"And I'm so afraid that these thoughts will threaten the contentment I've enjoyed for years as a single woman. I believe I've been a good steward in this area.

Listen, when I go to church, it's to worship, to serve and to receive the Word. I have no carnal, ulterior motive, do you understand?"

"Yes, my sister, I understand."

"I've known such peace and liberty without that kind of desperation. God gave me this gift, and I've never known Him to be an Indian-giver! So, we just need to touch and agree that this attack from the enemy will go back to the pit of hell. I still have much work to do."

Jean fingered the eternity band on her left hand and gently said to her friend, "Nola, did you ever consider that maybe your gift of singleness was seasonal and not permanent? You always said that you'd be open to remarry if it was God's will for you. What if marriage is what would bring God glory in this season of your life?"

Now it was Nola's turn to stare blankly at Jean.

Finally she replied, "What are you saying, that God wants me to marry now, at 55 years old? Jean, who on God's Earth would I marry? There is no one around that I am at all interested in, no one who is even… suitable."

"Nola, are you're saying that these thoughts are not focused on any individual?"

"That's correct, Jean. I can't even name or identify a person."

Help me Jesus, Jean prayed to herself before responding.

"Nola, I don't claim to understand what's going on, but I'm not going to worry because I trust God and His faithfulness. Tell me, if the situation was reversed and I came to you, how would you respond?"

At first Nola hesitated.

"Well…" Jean pressed.

"Alright, I'd suggest that we go before the Lord and inquire of Him.

Jean smiled. "I know you would and now you should expect no less from me."

"You've been a Friend" had just begun to play. Jean rose to turn the music off but decided to turn up the volume instead. The awesomeness of God, expressed in those lyrics took them to a place of humble meditation.

Before long, Nola and Jean were on their feet, each one lifting up their own praise with gladness and thanksgiving. Then, the supplications came forth.

About an hour later, Nola said goodnight to her friend and went to bed with a renewed assurance that God's love would always prevail over fear.

Well, those thoughts ceased to trouble Nola. Yes, they had required a response but not an immediate acceptance or denial. When her response was to seek the will of God and trust in Him instead of making assumptions, the anxiety was disarmed.

The weeks that followed were filled with deliberate Spirit-filled worship. This shifted her focus to God's declaration in Jeremiah 29:11. She could stand firm on the integrity of His plan for her future.

If the thoughts were of God, they could not be rebuked and would manifest at the appointed time. On the other hand, if this was a distraction come to test her, well that too would be revealed.

She had ministered these truths to countless other women through the years. But this experience caused her to understand how ministers can be hindered by their failure to yield and receive ministry, just as teachers can be hindered by an unwillingness to be taught.

God's loving conviction is such a comfort. In the time of need, His word in us will spring up to everlasting life.

Inner peace was not the only fruit of Nola's rekindled passion for worship. Time spent in God's presence brought forth a new book. *Dwelling* (inspired by Acts 17:28) would be her second poetic offering, combining Scripture, prayers, and narratives. After a year of edits and revisions, the text was finally ready.

Nola's women's conference in Dallas put the project on a brief hold, but she returned home ready to proceed. Just one last component had to be addressed. This book would be illustrated. In addition to the cover design, Nola had been given visualizations for each of the three chapters.

She began to pray that God would send someone who could interpret her sketches so that they spoke from the pages of the book.

About two weeks later, a call came from her editor, Ezra Hill. He had found her illustrator, the one appointed by God for this project. According to him, it was as good as done! Nola arranged to meet Ezra the next day. She was grateful for another prayer answered and could hardly wait to hear the details over lunch.

Solomon's Porch was one of Nola's favorite spots, and her first choice for a working lunch. The sidewalk café transformed itself each weekend into a rich outpouring of creative Christian expression. It was the place to go for anointed music, drama, and the spoken word. She arrived early and requested an outside table.

The urban landscape before her was a testimony in itself. Nola took in the sights, thanking God for breathing new life into what was once a ravaged neighborhood. How similar her life was to this hometown of hers.

Many of the art pieces that adorned her home were purchased next door at Salt and Light Images, which also sold lovely, handcrafted jewelry. The Living Manna Reading Room had just opened across the street. She would use that venue to launch the book signing tour for *Dwelling*.

Nola knew the One who had raised her up, giving her beauty for ashes, and she was not about to deny His name. It was Jesus who ordered her footsteps putting the right people in her path just when she needed them.

Ezra Hill was one of those appointed people. *Blood Bath* and *Wholly His* could not have become best sellers without him. He was that literary objective eye, so needed in the final stages of delivery. Every baby is wonderful to the parent, even when covered in after-birth. But, it takes a gentle skill to clean that baby up and hand it back, ready for viewing.

"Hello, Nola, how are you?" Ezra smiled, rushing to the table.

"I'm just fine Ezra, how are you?"

"Marvelous and hungry, my sister," was his reply as he sat down and became engrossed in the menu before him.

Nola leaned forward to reclaim his attention.

"I'm really looking forward to hearing about this artist. I know the illustrations were unexpected, but they had come to me during the writing process and I had no peace until I decided to include them. I hope I'm making sense?"

"Yes, Nola, I'm with you and I know this brother will be able to deliver."

"Well, come on, Ezra, tell me something about him, what has he done and how soon will he be available?"

"Well, here's the thing, his name is Seth Jordan, but he doesn't know that this is his assignment, not yet anyway. As a matter of fact, he doesn't even know about your illustrations."

"What do you mean he doesn't know? Didn't you tell him about the project?"

"Not exactly Nola, I met him at the Christian Writer's Retreat in Myrtle Beach…the one you couldn't make."

"Yes, well I still haven't figured out how to be in two places at once Ezra. As you know I had the Sheroes of Faith Conference in Dallas this year."

"Understood, understood my sister, but you were missed. Anyway, Seth was there with some of his original art. Nola, only someone who has been through the fire could produce such beauty.

He's read your books; he said they really blessed him. I gave him your card, here is his. Now let's eat."

Ezra motioned for the waiter.

The café delivered its usual splendid service, but Nola barely noticed. As her eyes moved back and forth from the business card to the man across the table, she was at a loss for acceptable words. So, she kept quiet and tried to focus on the perfectly prepared curried chicken salad on crunchy ciabatta.

Ezra wolfed down his salmon croquettes over cheddar grits, all the time mumbling something about how he was just the messenger assigned to put her and Seth in contact with one another.

"This project was ordained from above," he cried, waving his fork in the air. "All you guys have to do is pick up the phone."

And, then, he had the nerve to interject, "If you don't believe me, ask the Holy Spirit!"

No, no, no, thought Nola, this lacks all the sense of order and decorum that she'd come to expect from Ezra. Didn't he call her and say that he had found her illustrator, and it was as good as done?

As good as done does not imply that the person still needed to be introduced to the idea and then sold on the actual project. Was God trying to tell her that she was wrong about including the illustrations after all?

"Just ask Him!" Ezra repeated, pointing upward.

Nola was about to ask her editor-friend for a moment of silence when her heart heard the words, *"Daughter, this is of Me."*

Nola wasted no time. She called Seth that evening.

Their initial conversation went surprisingly well, effortless on her part. Seth seemed a little nervous but very glad to hear from her. "I – you were missed at the Christian Writers' Retreat. I told Ezra how much your books have blessed me. I'm delighted that you called!"

"Well, I praise God for His kindness towards me and I thank you for the encouragement. I'm sorry I missed your exhibit. The retreat is promoted on my website, and I believe in its mission but, this year, I had another assignment."

"Oh, I can relate and I applaud your obedience. By the way, *Daughter in Waiting* is a great website. Men should not be thrown by the *Daughter* reference. I've learned so much from your online Bible studies."

"Thanks again, Seth. Although I am a minister who is female, my Bible studies are gender inclusive. I find myself reminding people of the "Daughter of Zion" reference used in Scripture to describe all of God's people.

In the same light, women should embrace their inheritance in Christ, referred to in Scripture as our adoption as sons through Jesus Christ. I'm always glad to hear that someone is being blessed by the ministry.

And speaking of blessings, Ezra was certainly impressed with your gift."

"Was he?"

"Yes indeed, as a matter of fact, that's why I'm calling. My next book is in need of an illustrator, and I'd like to present the project to you. Actually, you have been highly recommended."

"Well, I can hardly wait!"

"Really, just like that?"

"My soul says yes, and I am honored. When are you free?"

After comparing calendars, they decided that Nola would fly to Charleston, South Carolina, Seth's current place of residence. As a writer, Nola had developed a crush on Charleston with its lovely palmetto trees and garden courtyards.

Sorely in need of some R&R, she was easily persuaded by Jean to add some downtime to her itinerary.

Nola took a late morning flight into Charleston. She had tentatively accepted Seth's invitation for a post-meeting dinner but declined his offer to pick her up at the airport. Time was needed alone, to unwind and prepare herself for the presentation.

She checked-in to the hotel and ordered room service. An unexpected three hour nap followed lunch. She awoke just in time to change and catch a cab to Seth's address which housed both his residence and commercial space.

Nola entered his studio and was blown away. Never had she seen such a collection of Christian art.

How can I show this man my measly pencil sketches?

Her first impulse was to turn and run but Nola had heard clearly. So she stood there, willing her flesh to be still.

"Seth, your work is amazing. God is glorified in each piece. I see why Ezra was so impressed."

"Thank you Nola, I'm truly grateful for God's grace. Please, let's sit." He escorted her over to a suede tufted sofa, and they took a seat.

"Seth, I studied fashion design in high school but, I'm no artist, so I hope you won't laugh." Nola gave a nervous chuckle, trying to steady her hands as she opened the portfolio.

Seth was genuinely surprised by her comment. *Lord, doesn't she know?*

"Nola, I respect your gift and I'd never make fun of your vision."

My ex-husband did. Nola recalled that time and closed her eyes as if to rebuke the memory.

"Are you okay?"

"Yes, I'm fine. Let me show you what I have."

Seth was amazed as she presented her drawings for the book cover and each of the three chapters. He could see the message in each piece and visualize the finished work.

"Thank you, Nola, for trusting me with this. I can have something for you very soon – say, in a week or so."

"Wow, that's wonderful. I had hoped that you would understand where I was coming from. I brought the text as well so that you could have a feel for the whole project."

"Thanks, I absolutely feel where you're coming from. Would you like to see each piece as it's completed?"

"Oh no, I'll wait until they're all done. I'm so grateful for your desire to take this on."

Neither had any doubts about the collaboration. After finalizing the contract and confirming their next appointment, Seth picked up the text and began reading some of her poetry.

This sparked a round of intense conversation about everything from discipleship to politics. Two hours later, dinner plans were cancelled by mutual agreement, and Nola returned to her hotel. Somehow they were both too full to eat.

Back at the hotel, Nola was glad to be alone with her thoughts. Seth's excited response to her sketches had been such a relief. But there was more to this brother than his art. He was a thinker, well-read, and interested in things that mattered.

His conversation had depth, but he never spoke to her in a condescending manner. Nola had seen a lot of ministries bogged down by the same male chauvinism that plagued corporate boardrooms.

Seth was a breath of fresh air during their conversation. They shared the same views on most of the issues discussed. When they disagreed over a particularly volatile issue, it was concluded that the two combined perspectives posed a more balanced view of the subject.

Even when iron got to sharpening iron, there was mutual respect and it was never boring. Seth and Nola merely agreed to disagree.

Still having no desire for food, Nola undressed and began to consider all that had been said and done since Ezra first mentioned Seth to her.

Other projects came to mind that were on hold because the design concept needed development. Maybe the season was at hand to revisit them? Finally, she remembered her initial supplication for an illustrator.

After a long massaging shower, Nola crawled into bed and prayed aloud.

"Abba Father, You would not give me a stone when I asked for bread. Lord, this is kingdom business. I do not sense danger here, but I offer all of it up to You. Give me wisdom and discernment.

Protect me from anything counterfeit and keep me within the boundaries of what You have ordained for me. Be glorified in all that is said and done. In the name of Jesus, I pray."

Almost immediately, she surrendered to a sweet sleep.

Nola felt no urgency to follow-up with Seth before the appointed time. Her project was in good hands.

After all, this was her first real vacation in almost two years. Falling into an easy laid back mode over the next few days, she slept-in and ordered room service without guilt.

When she ventured out, Nola was quite comfortable in her own skin wandering about the city of Charleston, taking in its beauty and history.

At a boardwalk café, she ordered a grilled shrimp and asparagus salad. She lingered there a long time just reflecting on the many ways her life had been renewed.

The old Nola's desperate need for companionship, and her fear of life-alone would have sapped all the joy from a solo vacation. But Jesus had set her free from all that bondage.

There were external changes as well. When hypertension struck the year before, Nola changed her eating habits and started an exercise program. It wasn't long before she began to see a newly toned reflection in the mirror.

Of course, she took full advantage of the hotel's fitness center. One day, after a brisk Zumba work-out, Nola had another serious craving for seafood. The concierge recommended a fine establishment down the street from the hotel.

Following a long luxurious bath, Nola lay across the bed for a minute considering what to wear. Smiling with anticipation, for no apparent reason, she got up and stood before the full length mirror in silent reflection. The ivory bath sheet was a striking adornment to her soft pecan coloring.

After perusing her wardrobe choices, Nola decided on a belted fit-and-flare coral dress with a bateau neckline. The knee length garment flattered her smooth bare legs. Peep-toe kitten heels revealed a flawless French pedicure.

Although tradition dictated shorter cuts for middle-aged women, Nola's hair stopped just past her shoulders. She piled her lustrous, natural tresses into a thick French roll, full at the crown. A single fire opal dangled from each ear as she exited the hotel and made her way to dinner.

Several admiring glances followed Nola as she entered the restaurant and was escorted to a comfortable back table with a window view. It never ceased to amaze her that she still turned heads. But years had passed since anyone had sparked her interest. The thought of that changing evoked mixed emotions. Was she ready and willing to be vulnerable again?

Nola's gave the waiter her request for starters. She looked around at the other tables, many occupied by couples.

How many of them were happy together, and what had they sacrificed not to be alone?

Just then she heard a light tap on the window. It was Seth.

Lord, where did he come from? What was there to do but motion for him to join her?

Wearing a slim lapel charcoal grey suit with a black shirt open at the collar, Seth received his own share of glances as he cut a path to her table. But, his eyes were fixed on Nola. He sat down and smiled that disarmingly gentle smile.

"Well, Seth, this is a nice surprise!"

"Yes, for me as well, I was headed home from a meeting, just about to get into my car when I spotted you from across the street."

Seth pointed out the window to his Volvo as if to confirm his story. Nola found his gesture amusing and not without charm.

"This was the only appointment on my calendar that could not be rescheduled. But, as of tomorrow morning the completion of your project will have my undivided attention. I'm almost done as a matter of fact."

"I'm not at all worried. I've been enjoying some much needed downtime."

Well, I guess he'd like to stay for dinner.

"Won't you join me for dinner?"

"I'd love to Nola, thank you."

The waiter brought Nola's appetizer and beverage. Seth requested a lime Perrier and a menu.

A brief silence ensued as they watched a large party try and sort out their bill. They had kept the bar quite busy and not one of them was seeing too straight. The waiter returned with Seth's request.

"So, how are you enjoying Charleston?"

"Oh, Seth, it's a lovely city. I can imagine how time spent on a gorgeous wrap around porch could inspire the writer in me. But, New York is still home and my brownstone stoop is very dear to my heart. Have you ever been?"

Seth's nervous expression made her regret the question.

"Actually yes, I was born there."

"Really, you were?"

"Yes, but I moved after my mother passed away."

Seth cleared his throat and emptied his water glass.

"Then I lived with my grandmother in South Carolina until I finished high school. Nola, the food here is really amazing. What have you decided to try?"

She gladly allowed Seth to change the subject.

"I think I'll go with the broiled rainbow trout."

"Great choice, I believe I'll have the same." The waiter

reappeared and took their orders.

Their eyes met often over dinner but they willed each glance to tread softly. Conversation was free of guile, despite a mutual flood of silent thoughts.

Does she know how beautiful she is? Her beauty does not intimidate; she is rare indeed.

This is a handsome man and he does not seem to know it. Everything about him is meekness personified. There is so much of him to take in.

Nola found herself wishing that she could stare without being rude. She was never good at remembering faces. She decided to engrave his image in her mind and revisit it later.

I'd say he's a cross between Hari Rhodes and Idris Elba...and he smells of Grey Flannel after shave.

So that's how the evening went.

The food was amazing as well, just as Seth had promised. After dinner and dessert, they took a very slow walk to her hotel. It ended too soon.

In the lobby, Seth thanked her again for the invitation to dine. Nola assured him that he was quite welcome.

He returned to his car well aware that something he'd presumed dead was beginning to stir again. Seth determined in his soul not to say a word in her presence without the leading of the Spirit. Then he drove his happy, hopeful self on home.

The *Dwelling* project was a labor of love and Seth completed the illustrations with ease. Nola's marriage of words and images was clearly God-inspired. Her creative narrative fueled his artistic response and provoked in him a new level of worship. At one point, he took a break and began to pray.

"Father, how and when do I tell her, or will You reveal it to her heart?"

It had only been two months since he'd found the poem in *Blood Bath* and wept. After that, he began to read her novel, *Wholly His*. One evening, after closing the book, Seth had a prophetic dream. It foretold of a continuous collaboration with the author.

But then came his disappointment, when she failed to show at the Writer's Retreat, followed by the elation of her phone call. The highs and lows had been overwhelming at times.

Nevertheless, an audacious hope had taken root in Seth's heart. It was not of his making, and it was destined to prevail. She had sought him out for this project, and he knew that was of God.

Seth couldn't help but wonder if his profound remembrance of decades past had been mutual. And now that she was here, would there also be the manifestation of mutual recognition?

"It's in Your hands, Father. Only time and love will tell."

With that, Seth returned to his project.

In the years following her divorce, Nola had sought to avoid situations that might defile or confuse her focus. But, her time with Seth had been pure fellowship. In his company, there was a peace not rooted in man. God had assured her that this collaboration was orchestrated by Him.

When she received His word at the café, it seemed so simple. Had she missed some of the meaning? Nola wondered about those old thoughts and where they had gone. Could they have been the shadow that comes before the reality is revealed?

What she found most intriguing was that Seth seemed familiar to her in a way that she could not articulate. Nola really wanted to be understood by this man, but she did not know why.

Their next scheduled meeting would be a working dinner at his home. Her anticipation was high regarding the finished product. She also looked forward to more time with the artist.

When the day arrived for the big reveal, Nola began her preparation from the time she awoke. Her meditation was on Luke 1:45, "Blessed is she who has believed that the Lord would fulfill his promises to her!"

Father let it be done according to your will – whatever it is.

Nola was much more relaxed as she entered Seth's home for the second time. She came bearing edible gifts. Seth relieved her of a fruit and cheese tray. She followed him into the kitchen with a bottle of sparkling mango cider.

Her eyes took in the floor plan of his home, and she was pleased. It was an artist's home, creative, and tastefully done. A double-sided fireplace served as the divider between the dining area and living room.

She looked around, recognizing things she'd never seen. Somehow they either paralleled or complemented her possessions. Many of the titles in his library could also be found in hers.

Nola decided that her brownstone could use a Seth Jordan piece. She made a mental note to work it into her budget in the near future.

As he busied himself in the kitchen, she volunteered to set the table. In no time, the two were sitting down to a feast of braised veal chops, petit Yukon gold potatoes and stir-fried kale. Besides being a gifted artist, Seth also knew his way around the kitchen.

Conversation was minimal, as they were busy with the food. After second helpings of the main course, they agreed that dessert would have to wait until later.

Now it was time for Seth to unveil the fruits of his labor. When the table was cleared away, he grabbed his laptop and pulled a chair around next to Nola's.

First, he showed her the cover for *Dwelling*, which visualized the believer's abiding life in Christ. He then pulled up each chapter illustration with its accompanying Scripture verse.

Not knowing whether to laugh or cry, Nola did a combination of both.

"Oh, Seth, these are so good. I mean they are great."

He had brought Nola's drawings to life in a way that exceeded her expectations. As a result of their efforts, *Dwelling* would edify her readers and God would be glorified.

She exclaimed to herself, "What more could any minister hope for?"

Seth's response was, "Come with me."

He led her by the hand into his studio where four covered easels stood. "Now, close your eyes for a second." Nola obeyed.

"Okay, you may open up."

She could not believe her eyes. The artist had put his interpretations on canvas. As a special gift, the writer would be going home with four one-of-a-kind Seth Jordan pieces! Nola smiled at him with a heart too full for audible words. Seth heard and was glad.

They decided to have dessert outside. His wrap-around porch was a relaxed space, comfortably furnished. Seth placed the cheese tray on a glass and bamboo table between two easy chairs. Nola refilled the glasses. Angella Christie's music flowed softly out from the living room. It was a lovely evening; the air was warm and sweet.

However, the beauty of an otherwise perfect setting was overshadowed by their concern for the future. *Dwelling* was virtually completed to everyone's satisfaction. But, where did they go from here?

Neither had a clear frame of reference to draw from after so many years of being alone. Both had come too far with God to even flirt with sin. They wanted to know what heaven had ordained for them. That was the question burning in their hearts.

"The brie is really good."

"Yes it is; I hoped you would enjoy it."

Two hearts echoed, *Holy Spirit, help us*.

Finally Seth was led to start.

"Nola, you're blessed to be walking in the call of God for your life and your writing suggests an awesome testimony. I'd love to hear the story of your journey if you'd care to share it."

From the beginning, Seth had spoken to Nola's spirit on a personal level, and she wanted to be open with him. Yes, her journey was a testimony. And there was a particularly pivotal moment in the molding of this vessel. She knew she'd have to start there.

"Seth, I'm divorced. I was married before."

Okay, maybe I shouldn't have blurted that out. But, she continued, willing fear away.

"During the initial separation, I actually prayed for reconciliation. I was willing to do what I thought would please God, despite my feelings. But when Jared, my ex-husband, refused counseling and filed for divorce, I determined that it was somehow working together for my good. As the enemy tried to condemn me with echoes of *God hates divorce*, I was strengthened by the truth that it was not the unpardonable sin.

I found a counselor on my own. The pain of betrayal soon lost its sting. Then, at some point after the final decree, I was led to revisit that relationship with fresh eyes. Sometimes God will take you back in order to bring you forward. He had some things to show me.

One day, I sat pondering Jared's deception with righteous indignation, (he'd committed adultery on our honeymoon). I was suddenly made aware of my own self-deception, which along with my low self-esteem, had led me to accept his marriage proposal in the first place.

You see, I didn't trust God to make a way for me. I failed to believe the word from one itinerant minister, who told me that the enemy would use Jared to try and destroy me because of my calling.

I didn't even know I had a calling. I was in a church that didn't recognize a calling in anyone without a master's degree and I had never completed my bachelor's.

Finally, there was the revelation of my failure to truly stand on faith during the marriage. I went through the whole experience crippled by fear and anger. Those two burdens dictated my every thought, word, and action.

But, the confession and repentance that followed the revelations freed me up in ways that I could not have imagined. I became a woman of prayer, submitted to the Potter's hand. That's when Jesus revealed the Father and His love for me.

That changed everything. I began the life-long journey of learning to surrender. A desire was birthed in me to somehow demonstrate a trust in Him that I had no frame of reference for.

And I could not get enough of God's word. His word became life to me. After a time, I was led to a church fellowship where the pastor was not bound by tradition. The door was opened for me to minister according to my gift and calling."

Throughout Nola's testimony, Seth maintained a steady, compassionate gaze. She finished her story and held her breath for his response.

What must he be thinking of me now?

"You're a chosen vessel, my sister. I am honored and grateful to know you."

It mattered that he spoke such words, and she smiled her sincere appreciation. He returned a smile that recalled another place and time.

Nola thought to herself, *I know that smile – it will come to me.*

Seth had shown himself to be a great listener, fully engaged, and non-judgmental. He possessed a God-tempered, masculine vulnerability. Nola wanted to ask him about his journey, but she remembered the discomfort her questions had caused before.

Maybe he will offer.

Seth was a wondrous secret in need of knowing. How she'd love to gain that knowledge!

"Nola, I'd like to tell you about myself, if you don't mind."

"Oh, I don't mind," she replied.

Now it was Seth's time to speak, and his words would pierce her heart.

"I too was married, but my marriage was dissolved by a different decree. We were returning home from a watch-night service at the church. I was driving and my wife was in the back seat with my son.

A drunk driver jumped the median and was coming straight at us. I tried to turn to avoid him but he plowed into my rear. I lost my wife the night of the crash. My son lived a few weeks and, then, I buried him. I barely had a scratch.

There was no sense to be made of it. The belief that they were in heaven did not take away my pain. I was far from heaven, and they were beyond my reach.

I kept asking God the same questions that seemed to fall on deaf ears… *How could they cease to exist for me, and how was I supposed to keep living without them?*

The pain was crippling. At some point, I talked myself out of suicide and settled for a living-death, instead.

Like a dog that returns to its own vomit, I began to seek comfort in the places I'd known before I knew Jesus. I found temporary pleasure but no peace. One hung-over morning, God spoke to me through a woman who had known me back in the day."

"Seth, you don't belong here with me."
"How do you know where I belong?"
"I know because I no longer recognize you."
"What's that supposed to mean?"
"It means you've been changed and you can't return to the person you were before Love changed you. Self-destruction is not a fitting tribute to the loved ones you lost. God left you alive for a reason."
"Humph, yeah right – for what reason?"
"That's for you to discover. When I come out of the shower, please be gone."

"That was nine years ago. It took a one-night stand for me to realize that I'd hit rock bottom with nowhere to go but up. My surrender was gut-wrenching and pitiful, but it was the first step toward a life worth living. Before long, the solitude of desolation was replaced by a healing intimacy. It was intensive care, God's way.

Nola, I thought I knew Him before tragedy invaded my life. But, it was through the ministry of loss that I was graced to enter into a deeper fellowship, not only the revelation of God as Savior, but God as Abba Father.

It's so true that Jesus came to show us the Father! That dimension had been missing, but it was sorely needed for my journey."

Nola nodded in agreement, saying, "How awesome is the revelation of Abba Father! It's the truth that overrides all the facts of our natural circumstances. Seth, were you saved when you met your wife?"

"Yes, after I finished high school in South Carolina, I returned to New York to attend Pratt, where I earned my degree. I then moved into a rundown Brooklyn tenement with a group of other starving artists. I guess you could call it an urban commune with all of us struggling to live our self-proclaimed dreams.

One evening, I gave in to my aunt's perpetual invitations to attend Bible study at her church. But, God spoke to my heart during the lesson. When the invitation was made, I confessed Jesus and believed.

I met Simone that night. She had gone to the altar as well. We eventually fell in love and got married. To this day, I'm very grateful for the balance of Biblical literacy and Spirit-filled worship offered at that church. It laid a good foundation for us."

Nola then asked two questions, not knowing why.

"Seth, when did you first discover your gift? Were you working as an artist when you lost your family?"

After a brief but awkward silence, Seth cleared his throat and addressed her second question.

"When Simone told me that I was about to become a father, I immediately pursued a more reliable means of support, full-time. God showed me favor as I transitioned pretty smoothly into IT marketing. We had some wonderful years together. Simone never asked me to lay aside my art, but she and Daniel always came first. My son's name was Daniel."

"Seth, providing for your family and making them a priority was God's plan for you at that time. He orchestrates the seasons in our lives."

"Yes, I had to learn about seasons. God rekindled my passion for art about seven years ago. But this time, it was focused and sanctified."

Then Seth heard Nola repeat the other question.

"So, when did you first discover your gift?"

Suddenly, Seth's hands were on fire. He rubbed them on his pants in a futile attempt at relief from the heat and moisture.

So it is now, Lord.

"I was a little nappy headed kid back in Bedford-Stuyvesant. It started with a box of crayons…many years ago. I'll be right back."

Oh my God! Nola thought, following Seth with her eyes as he rose and disappeared into the house.

He returned with his copy of *Blood Bath*, sat back down, and picked up the conversation as if he'd never left.

"Actually, a very wise preacher woman put it like this."

Seth opened to the piece entitled, "First Knight Eulogy." He began a slight back and forth rocking motion as he read her narrative, prayer, and poem.

Who was the little boy that crossed my path so long ago?
So meek and lowly, he gave his all and was rejected.

Thank you Jesus for a truth once hidden but now revealed.
He was "The least of these."
And so in remembrance,
I record this first knight eulogy.

First Knight Eulogy
His name I never knew
"Boston Blacky" they called him
I tried to buy crayons one day
But my coins were short
He was there, beautiful and unkempt
I returned home and forgot.

He smiled at me when I came to the door
All rags, except for those brand new Crayolas
Daddy teased, so I had to refuse
I never saw him again –
Not with my eyes.

Nola held her breath as Seth closed the book and continued to speak. He smiled that lovely smile but his eyes were ever so glassy.

"I had just cashed in my empty soda bottles at the candy store."

Nola was on her feet now. Moving to the porch balcony, she grabbed the rail and looked down at his garden. Leaning her head on the column, she tried to slow her heartbeat. Seth followed and stood behind her. His breath on her neck and the scent of his presence somehow sustained her. He continued.

"I wanted to feel the coins in my hands a while before I made my candy selection, you see. But, you came in to buy those crayons, and Mr. Henry said you were 10 cents short. Nola, all I wanted at that moment was for you to have those crayons.

After you left, I made the purchase and sat on my stoop until I got up the nerve to march my raggedy pants over to your house. I already knew where you lived.

I used to follow you home after school sometimes – at a distance of course. When you walked with your head cast down it caused your braids to fall across your face. Then when you'd look up suddenly they'd swing around. You were always a pretty sight to me."

Nola turned to him and backed away for a full view of his six foot frame.

He continued. "I never forgot your sad expression, as you closed the door in my face, with your dad laughing behind you. I ran home trying to understand how I had brought sadness to someone I wanted to make happy. So, there I was with no candy and this stupid box of crayons."

A boyish grin replaced the smile but his eyes were still moist.

"Having no other outlet for the hurt that defined my daily existence, I started to draw. It quickly became my refuge. Soon, I began to incorporate regular pencil drawings into my compositions.

Before long, my teacher, Miss Walker, started to notice. She introduced me to other tools and mediums, often at her own expense. My teachers, in South Carolina, were just as supportive.

They, along with my grandmother, encouraged me to begin entering contests. Of course, I was the *fly in the buttermilk* at most of the competitions, but that didn't stop me from winning some. After high school, I attended Pratt on a full scholarship."

Once more, it was Nola's turn to speak.

"Almost every kid in the neighborhood was poor. I stayed home from school when there was no milk money. Some nights, our supper was hog head cheese and saltines. But, there was always someone poorer. Mess flows downhill and the poorest got picked on the most. Seth, you were the poorest. I hated the way they talked about you, but I was afraid to say so.

Yes, I remember the dark and lovely boy in the tattered clothes, who smiled at me when I walked into the candy store. And, I never forgot your smile as you offered me your sacrifice and was rejected.

It's no excuse, but I didn't want my father to tease me about having a boyfriend. Even after I refused your gift, he still teased and it made me feel dirty. He was like that.

What you saw was a sad and serious little girl, easily shamed. But, even then I regretted the way I treated you. After that, I never saw you around the block; you just disappeared."

"Well, Nola, I did my best to avoid you. Then, my mother got sick the following year, and I had to stay with my cousins. She never came home from the hospital. That's when I moved to South Carolina."

"I'm so sorry, Seth."

Nola moved closer. She searched his face, her eyes lingering on every detail.

"I remembered that you were beautiful, but I could not recall your exact features. When I gave my life to the Lord, I was a little girl of 36, with many unresolved issues. As I drew closer to God, the memory of that day, so long ago, became more intense, and it remained with me.

I often wondered if you had survived into manhood, and I prayed that you were somewhere alive and happy. There was no way to find you. I never even knew your real name.

But, when I began writing my first book, I knew that you would be a part of it somehow."

Seth drew nearer and she did not back way. He took her hand.

"First Knight Eulogy" is an interesting title. It took a minute for me to understand."

"Yes, most people associate eulogies with funerals, but to eulogize means to give a good testimony about someone."

Nola then offered a heartfelt confession.

"Seth Jordan, you were my one and only true knight, and I want to thank you. God has shown me a great kindness. He has allowed me to see your face again and tell you how I feel."

Their eyes locked as if to drink each other in. Then, they reached for one another, ignoring the vastness of their separation. You see, they were reaching to bridge five decades of a hope-differed.

Seth embraced her with a righteous humility, thankful for the God of a second chance. He gently kissed her hair and whispered, "Never say, never."

Nola closed her eyes, buried her head in his chest, and wept for joy.

The End

(I mean)

The Beginning.....

Offerings

*"Then the LORD said to Cain,
'Why are you angry? Why is your face
downcast? If you do what is right,
will you not be accepted...?'"*
~Genesis 4:6-7

Offerings

Five-year-old Ramona was trying her best to keep her two-year-old brother from the half empty beer can.

"No, Rory, that's a grown folk's drink. I'll find your bottle."

The two children jumped to attention at the sound of their mother's voice. Faith did not play.

"You kids better shut up in there or you won't be going nowhere tomorrow!"

Faith's tone immediately softened as she turned her attention to her male friend. "This is our time tonight, right Babe?"

Babe, better known as Rock, was Faith's flavor of the month – at least she was hoping for a month. Rock sat spread-legged, twisting his dreads, and thinking that if it wasn't for the child support, which he knew she'd just received, he'd walk out.

But, he deserved something for putting up with Faith the past few days and he was going to have it. The B Club was live tonight, and she was paying.

He replied, "Yeah, this is our night, all the way."

Faith Best (known most recently as Effie to her friends) was old for her 29 years, and it was beginning to show. She sat before the cluttered card table, which served many functions: dining table, TV stand, and ironing board, to name a few. Tonight, it was a vanity table for the woman of many sorrows.

"How did I agree to this mess anyhow? I got to go sit up in somebody's church at 11:00 o'clock in the morning for some preacher to pray over Rory. I got prayed over, Mona got prayed over, and what good did it do anything?

And, next month they want me to go to some women's conference to hear my sister tell somebody else how to live, like I didn't know her when. Dang, I'm just not feeling it, Babe."

Babe checked his watch and nodded his agreement.

After three Hard Lemonades, staring into the hand mirror was causing Faith's head to spin. The lip gloss seemed to be missing the outline of her mouth no matter how hard she tried.

"My sister should be here any minute now, Babe. Mona and Rory, get your shoes on, Auntie Gabi is on the way."

Faith got up and somehow managed to step into her 4 inch heels. But, trying to smooth a size 6 mini skirt over her size 8 hips caused her to fall back in the chair with a thud.

"Oops, I tripped," she giggled.

This caused Faith's halter top to shift, sending her cleavage into illegal limits. But, she didn't notice, and Rock didn't care. The devil had already assured Effie that she looked good in everything she wore.

Just then, the doorbell rang, and both kids raced from the back room to the door.

"Get back here – acting like you never had no training. Babe, would you get the door please?"

Rock got up and opened the door, sitting back down like he'd over exerted himself. Gabi walked in and knelt to hug her niece and nephew. They returned the love.

"Hello, Faith," Gabi smiled up at her sister.

"Oh, Effie is just fine, thanks," she slurred ever so slightly. This here is my new friend, Rock."

"Hi, Rock."

"Hey," he replied, scanning Gabi's tastefully clad assets. Gabi caught it, so did Faith, resenting her sister even more.

"Listen, Faith, why don't I just keep the kids with me, at Momma's house, and you meet us at the church?"

"Whatever, Gabi. Their things are still in there on the bed. Meanwhile, I got someplace to be."

Gabi went into the bedroom and gathered the clothes she'd bought and dropped off that morning. When she came out, Faith had eased into her coat with Rock's half-hearted assistance. Gabi helped her niece and nephew into their jackets.

"Okay, let's haul on out everybody. Come here babies and give Mommy some sugar. See you tomorrow at the church."

Out on the street, the sisters went their separate ways in different directions.

The next morning, Pastor Blackmon flipped the script so that the visitors to Salt and Light Fellowship Church did not miss his sermon. The dedication service took place after the message was preached.

When the invitation was given for families to come forward, Rock started from the back of the church with Faith. However, upon reaching the third row, he plopped down and spent the whole ceremony scratching at his beard and trying not to yawn.

Meanwhile, the dejected club-weary mother joined her family and managed to get through the motions on cue.

Sadly, Faith was not up there sticking out like anybody's sore thumb. Gathered with her was a host of other clueless parents, some of them in their teens. But, also gathered were the faithful elders of each clan, determined to hang in there for the babies.

Gabi and Momma were constantly praying not only for Rory and Ramona but for all the little ones. Only Jesus could defy the odds and override the turmoil that defined their lives.

After Rory's dedication, everyone went back to Momma's house for Sunday dinner where Gabi had prepared a delicious meal of pot roast, turnip greens, yellow rice, and candied yams.

When Rock had stuffed himself to capacity, he motioned to Faith. She had business to handle before they could leave. However, the unsuspecting business partner was about to complicate things by leaving the room.

"Well, children, I think I need to lie down for a minute. Rock, it was nice to meet you."

"Ah, yes ma'am," he replied.

Rory and Ramona went over to kiss their grandmother as Rock gave Faith a nudge under the table.

"Momma, let me help you to bed. Gabi, I'll wash the dishes if you clear the table."

Gabi sensed that there was an ulterior motive for Faith's thoughtfulness. As Rock shuffled nervously in his seat, she went down the hall to listen outside her mother's door.

"I just need $50. My rent is short this month. I know you can spare it, Momma, if not for me, then for your grandkids."

"I don't believe you;" Gabi burst in. "How can you? Momma is on a fixed income and you stand there with your hands stretched out. I see at least $200 worth of tattoos on your boobs and arms. They aren't a month old."

"For your information, I didn't even pay for them, Miss Know-It-All."

"Oh, you paid for them, my sister, you laid and paid."

"Okay, enough you two!" The elder woman silenced her

daughters and reached for the change purse under her pillow.

"Here's the money, child. Faith, please try and budget a little better next month."

"Sure thing, Momma, I'll bring the babies back over real soon. And, I'll take care of those dishes now."

Ella Best closed the bedroom door behind her baby girl and turned to her first born.

"Now, Gabriella, there was no need for that."

"Sorry, Momma, but it's the truth."

"Even so, you know Jesus, she does not. To whom much is given, much is required."

When Gabi returned to the kitchen, Faith was frantically rushing to finish the dishes while looking over at Rock, who had just become $50 richer. As he sat checking his iPhone, she feared that he'd grow impatient and leave without her.

That scene took Gabi back to her past and rekindled a loving compassion for her sister. If she could only reach her!

"So how did you like the message today?"

"Oh, please Gabi! What a waste of time talking about bowing down to an unseen God. I'll save my worship on bended knees before a man that I can see, touch, and feel. And, if I treat him right, he will be mine one day. Why trust a God to deliver when I know what I want and how to get it my own self?"

Leaning closer to Gabi she whispered, "Rock is so fine and whatever it takes, I intend to keep him."

"Faith, you say that about everyone that comes along and it always ends in disappointment."

"You know what, Gabi? I've had enough of you and Momma for one day. I've fulfilled my motherly duty at that church, and I may or may not see you at your little preachin' debut. Now, it's time for me, my Boo, and my kids to leave. Don't judge me Gabi. Nobody's perfect – not even you!"

"Okay, I'll drive you home, Faith."

"The name is Effie, that's my name 'cause it suits me!"

The next night, Faith was looking forward to some more time with Babe. The kids had finished their Happy Meals and would soon be asleep.

Suddenly, Rock got a text message. "Oh no, baby, I got to tip out for a spell. Something jumped off with my boy over on Marcy!"

"No, please Rock, the kids are almost sleeping. Can't you stay a while? Just hold me if nothing else?"

Rock looked at her like she had lost her mind.

"Just hold you – if nothing else? You know what? You getting a little too clingy for me. This is why me and my baby's momma couldn't make it. A real man can't be boxed in like that. Why can't you women see that? Listen, I'll catch you later."

And Rock was in the wind.

Now Faith was a ball of unrighteous indignation, cussing and fussing as she cleared away the empty McDonald's bags and gathered up the mounds of crab leg shells from her dinner with Rock. Her best attempt at straightening up the place was when she had something else on her mind.

"I don't have to keep takin' this mess. He ain't the only one that wants me. I give him my body and my love. Tonight, I spent my doggone cable money on these crab legs he wanted so much and what do I get for it?

I give to my kids, and they don't even have anything to give back! All I do is give and what do I ever get? Mona and Rory, you better be fast asleep when I come in there!"

Finally, exhausted from another round of self-pity, Faith curled up in the fetal position across the room from her sure 'nuff babies and stared into the darkness.

"I'll hold you, Mommy," called Ramona softly.

"That's okay, Mona, Mommy's okay."

But the girl-woman turned her face to the wall, anointing her pillow with bitter tears.

The Sheroes of Faith Women's Conference was less than two weeks away, and Gabi was still not at peace with her message. It was good, but she wanted God's best. Nola Jordan, the conference leader, would expect no less from her sister-in-Christ.

Gabi first met Nola when she brought her Daughter in Waiting Workshop to Salt and Light Fellowship Church. Gabi came up for prayer, and Nola laid hands on the young woman, confirming everything Gabi had been hearing in her time alone with God.

Jesus would use that altar call to usher her into service. She received God's anointing and a new sense of purpose. At Not by Works Ministries, Nola began to mentor Gabi so that her gifts could be used in keeping with her calling. And now, a year later, Gabi would stand before God's women to deliver a message from Him.

Returning to her laptop, Gabi lifted a silent prayer. *Lord I'm your vessel, please show me what will glorify you and edify the women.*

God's response to her heart was short and sweet. *Tell your story, daughter.*

Almost immediately Gabi's soul was flooded with virtue and she began again.

The turnout for the conference surpassed everyone's expectations. Folding chairs were placed down the aisles of the sanctuary. When the psalmist finished a rousing rendition of "What I've been through," Nola Jordan read a portion of Scripture from The Parable of the Prodigal Son in Luke 15.

Gabi was up next. Her heart raced as she approached the platform. Looking out at the women whom God loved so much made her marvel at His election. It was a humbling experience to think that He had actually raised her up to proclaim His word – she of all people!

After scanning the pews more closely, Gabi finally saw her sister. Faith was way back in the corner, sitting with Lois, her occasional squeeze. The two women used same-sex recreation as a salve for the hurt and a vent for the anger that defined their existence.

It was all over with Rock. He had lost his apartment and, instead of moving in with Faith, he moved in with his baby's momma, who was pregnant again. As a result of this latest drama, Faith, (aka Effie) was blowing up her Facebook page with curses aimed at the whole male population. They'd all be worthless in her eyes – that's until the next one came along.

She and her friends never connected the dots between their problems and the choices they continued to make. Personal accountability was unheard of in her circle.

Nevertheless, on this day, Faith and Lois had come to church, and Gabi's heart was glad to see them.

Gabi opened up with a bold exhortation. "Good morning, saints and friends. Let the redeemed of the Lord say so! Psalm 107:2 says that the redeemed of the Lord ought to tell their story. And that's what I've been called to do in your hearing."

Then, Gabi prayed and obediently began her message.

"I had my last abortion before I'd ever heard the Gospel. I knew nothing about God's love. I didn't know that He knew me before He knit me together in my mother's womb.

After receiving the pregnancy test results, I thought back to my first abortion, a decade before, and wanted to scream. I remembered lying spread eagled on the table when it was over, straining my head to see the little bloody mass in the container. I could not understand my sudden desire to push the nurse aside and reclaim what the doctor had just suctioned out of me.

Afterwards, I limped on home feeling twice violated, first by the one who had poured in, and then by the one who drew out.

I dreaded the fact that it was happening all over again."

Gabi swallowed hard, leaned into the podium, and continued.

"In the ten years since my first pregnancy, I had gotten older but no wiser. All I knew was that another dream of love and happiness had fallen apart, leaving me alone and discarded.

Every time a relationship failed, I couldn't wait to patch myself up and get back out there to soothe my pain with someone new. After all, if I could make the next one work, I would show everyone who was keeping score that I had finally won. And, my worth as a woman would at last be validated.

I always ending up with men, who looked different on the outside, but, they had one very important thing in common. For these men, getting a woman pregnant against her will gave them a sense of power. At some point they'd jump me when my contraception was not in. Duh! If I could have seen them by the Spirit, I would have understood. But, I was in darkness myself."

At that comment Nola Jordan smiled up at Gabi and mouthed the words, "It's okay."

"This was my second forced pregnancy and I was tired. After making my appointment, I sat there on the bathroom floor with a bottle of Excedrin PM and considered ending it all.

I thought to myself, *What if I never find love with a man of my own? Why go on living? And why give another stranger the right to take my baby? Better we just die together.*

But, in the end, I was too much of a coward to have the baby, and too much of a coward to die with him or her."

As Gabi continued her story, she could tell from the varied reactions of the women, who had been there and who had not.

"Nevertheless, the Lord is rich in mercy and there is grace to repent. I am a witness. In spite of my loathsome sin, He had plans for me, and those plans did not include suicide.

His plans involved a future and a hope. God would lovingly show me that my problem was not with life because I was not living. I was simply one of the walking dead. You see, there is no life apart from God. After bringing me to that realization, He'd then go on to offer me His gift of life."

At that point Gabi took a brief digression from her notes.

"And let me say this, when Jesus raises you up out of the muck and the mire, He knows how to customize your healing because He was right there through the wounding.

Before I came to the Lord, I was a little girl who felt out of place in a woman's body. I'd stare longingly at families that seemed happy. But, instead of wanting to be that wife or that mother, I wanted to be that little girl who appeared to be safe, loved, and protected. Because I never had the loving care of an Earthly father, God had to start at the beginning and build me up.

But, ladies, as I surrendered to Him, He made a woman out of me! He made me a Godly woman and a vessel of honor. I can't put into words the blessed relief it is just to trust Him with my life.

God's plan for me is born of His perfect love and His flawless will. Please understand, I have not fully arrived or obtained. It takes a lifetime. But, this journey of faith is what being a *Daughter in Waiting* means to me."

That testimony got an "Amen," from Nola. As her mentor nodded in agreement, Gabi continued.

"I understand that my 35 years of life have been in preparation for this moment. God lifted me up, not just so that I could live a blessed life, but so that I could offer the Giver of this blessed life to other hurting women.

This is not an offering of money and riches. It's an offering of salvation: eternal life, love, peace of mind, joy, hope, purpose, the realization of your true worth, and the gift of freedom in its purest sense. It is unfettered access to His loving arms of compassion and to His loving conviction, depending on your need at the time.

It sounds so good to me; I tend to ask myself at times, who wouldn't want that? But, I understand that this gift I speak of, and the invitation I offer may not be accepted by everyone gathered here tonight.

I know what some of you are asking yourselves. *How do I know if this is for me?*

Well, if you're sitting there thinking that I have made no sense to you at all, this may not be your time to surrender. If you still think that all you need is to find the right man, or the right woman, or the right job, then the offer is probably not for you just yet.

If the pretty darkness you're sleeping with looks like light to you, then you are still deceived. If you're persuaded that the right shade of MAC, nail tips, hairweave, or curl pattern, will make your life better and chase your blues away, this is probably not your day.

So then, whose hour of redemption is at hand? Well, before I could be lifted up, I had to go all the way down and acknowledge my situation for what is really was.

I believe this offer is for those who have reached their private pig's pen experience. It's for those who have realized that the touch and smell of slop are the makings of your dwelling.

But, you also finally realize that you don't belong there anymore! You're like an illegal alien, wallowing with the swine, when the Father has an inheritance waiting for you.

For those who have hit rock bottom and have come to the end of themselves, I have Good News. There is nowhere to go but up, if you will just arise.

Understand beloved, you can't make yourself worthy of God's salvation. Jesus did that on the cross."

At that point Gabi left the platform and stood in front of the center aisle. There she began her altar call.

"In the Parable of the Prodigal Son, the father did not go and pull his son out of the whore house because it would have been a premature intervention. Those do not last.

No, the son had to go through the process of spending all he had on false dreams and temporary pleasures before he spiraled down into the pig's pen.

The Bible does not say how long he wallowed down there before coming to his senses. But, at some point, he arose and started back home where the father was there to meet him on the road.

So, where are you today, beloved? Is this your time to arise? Is the Spirit speaking to your heart, calling you to come? If so, the altar is open.

I don't know your story or your specific need. Some may need salvation and some may need rededication. But, I do know that whatever you're in need of, the Blood of Jesus and His finished work on the Cross are more than enough. Jesus saves to the utmost and is able to keep those who are His. He has promised never to forsake us."

At that point, wailing began to erupt from certain women around the room. And, then, the Spirit-led procession to the altar began. Gabi and the other servants of God met every woman that came forth and began to minister according to each situation.

Meanwhile, Effie sat there seething with anger, gagging Faith within her ravaged soul.

"I can't believe this mess! I came here to expose Miss Thing's holier-than-thou behind before all these self-righteous haters. I just can't win with her. Come on, Lois, we got some place to be."

But, when she looked over at her friend in the next seat, something was radically wrong. No, Lois was not looking right by her estimation. Suddenly, up from Lois' belly erupted this ugly cry, and then she took off down the aisle to the altar.

There, Gabi prayed with Lois as she gave her heart to Jesus. But, Gabi's baby sister left the church that day, alone and unchanged.

Over the next few months, it became clear that God was joining Nola and Gabi together for ministry, like Paul and Timothy. When the opportunity arose for Nola to take the Sheroes of Faith Women's Conference on the road again, Gabi was asked to participate as a workshop facilitator.

Richmond would be the first stop on the itinerary followed by Fayetteville and Atlanta.

On the eve of their departure, Momma Ella hosted a pot-luck send-off that was well attended, except for the one, who was truly missed. Lois came but not Faith.

No one had actually seen Faith since the day Gabi preached. She'd moved out of her apartment with no forwarding address. Every effort to reach her by phone was countered by a semi-coherent voice message accusing the church hypocrites of stealing her BFF away. And no, she was not coming to any send-off celebration!

Gabi rose early the morning of her departure. Wanting to allow plenty of time to make their flight, she had the car loaded by 8:00 a.m. Just as she hopped behind the wheel and turned the ignition key, a shadow came up on her passenger side. Gabi jumped out of the vehicle and almost gasped at the sight. It had been seven months since she'd last seen her sister. The downward spiral had clearly been expedited.

Oh, Lord, maybe now she has nowhere to go but up.

A shaky, disheveled Faith stood there with Ramona at her side while Rory in her arms failed to conceal a third child on the way.

"How are you, Faith? Hello there, Rory and Mona."

"Hi, Auntie," was the sweet refrain that never failed to pierce Gabi's heart. She moved to embrace them, but her sister backed away, looking her up and down with contempt.

"Well, I guess I lost and you won again. But, how could you ever lose, being Momma's favorite and God's chosen at the same time? The only one that favored me was Daddy, and you know he favored me too good!"

"Faith, Daddy was an equal opportunity abuser."

"So you say!"

"Please come inside the house Faith; the kids are shivering."

"There you go, I get out my bed to see you off when I should be just turning over and all you can do is criticize me."

It was obvious that she and her babies had not seen a bed.

"I'm not criticizing, but it's warm inside and Momma would love to see you all."

"Well, I don't want to see her. I'm just here to prove that even though you brought me down, I ain't no sore loser is all."

"Oh, Faith, I did not bring you down, and I am not your enemy. Your battle has never been with me, except in your mind. And Momma has never had a favorite.

As for God, each day you are given is evidence of His love for you. Offer yourself to Him! God's love is nothing like the selfish, fickle, perversions of the people you've bowed down to or been used by.

I can't predict the future. I'm not called to judge anything before its appointed time, and neither should you. I hope that one day you'll realize how much you are loved – and always will be."

As Gabi walked back around to her car door, a defiant Faith put her son down to lift both hands in mocked praise.

"Oh, let's hear it for the Amen corner. Well, Effie don't need you or Momma! I can go over to Natesha's place right now – 'cause she owe me."

Then casting her eyes down to her swollen belly, she declared, "No, Rodney, he the one that sho 'nuff owe me!"

The older sister drove away in tears praying aloud, "Lord, if it be your will, please send her a word that she can relate to."

As Gabi's tail lights disappeared, the homeless mother gathered her precious, neglected babies and started back to nowhere.

After walking a few blocks, Rory had fallen asleep and Faith was overwhelmed by his weight. They stopped to rest on the stoop of an abandoned building. A brightly colored mural had been painted over its crumbling brick wall.

"Mommy, look at the pretty pictures."

"Mona, leave me alone please. Mommy don't feel well, you hear?"

"Yes, Mommy, I'm sorry… but what do the words say?"

"What words, Mona?"

"Those words in the picture, please tell me the words, Mommy."

"Okay, Mona, okay!"

Through her haze Faith followed the path of Mona's outstretched hand. She stared at the graffiti, straining her eyes to focus. Slowly, the message emerged.

Effie recoiled from the words Faith whispered – truth uttered softly by a sovereign grace.

"I can't hear you, Mommy. What do the words say?"

Faith looked down at her children, seeing them for the first time. Their beauty amazed her.

"The words say, 'God is love. Jesus saves.'"

Selah...

Gongs and Cymbals

"If I speak in the tongues of men or of angels, but do not have love, I am only a resounding gong or a clanging cymbal."
~1 Corinthians 13:1

Gongs and Cymbals

Pastor Gordon Riche, his wife Lorraine, and their two daughters were living the good life. Kingdom Glory Temple, the ministry started nearly a decade ago, was not yet a mega sized congregation. However, its inevitable growth had been confirmed by visiting apostles and prophets alike.

And until that manifestation took place, Pastor Riche vowed to call those things that are not, as though they were. For Gordon Riche and his particular circle of clerics, it was no secret what could be done by those who were willing to grab hold of God's word… and milk it for all its worth!

In fact, the milking of the word and the fleecing of the sheep had helped put the Riche clan in a lovely home with four luxury cars. The parking lot at Kingdom Glory Temple housed two double spaced gazebos designated for the first family. Gazebo I was referred to as *Bentleys One and Two for the Kingdom*. Gazebo II was referred to as *Beamers Three and Four for the Kingdom*. The Riche names were painted in gold on the reserved parking signs.

Every member of Kingdom Glory Temple had been assured that as they continued to bless the man of God, their own blessing would one day run down like oil from Aaron's beard. For as the head goes, so does the body. This concept was embodied in Kingdom Glory Temple's *Vision for Giving* statement of beliefs.

Any challenge to the tokens of honor bestowed on the First Family was treated as an act of rebellion. After all, if left unchecked, such behavior would stop the flow of blessing to the whole. Although the flow of blessing never seemed to make it past the front rows (reserved for the church board), most of the congregation accepted Kingdom Glory's doctrine as truth. And so, an atmosphere of unity and control prevailed for years.

But, for the past few months, Pastor Riche had begun to sense that something was wrong. His ability to work up the crowd seemed to be slipping. The people did not appear as happy with his sermons. This was frustrating to the preacher who had always emphasized style over substance.

When bodies hit the floor at Kingdom Glory Temple, it was due to the coercive power of man, not the Spirit of God. Now there seemed to be a famine of slain bodies. Altars empty of slain bodies might be an indication that the people were beginning to think for themselves. A thinking congregation could eventually lead to empty offering baskets. This thing needed to be nipped in the bud!

Kingdom Glory Temple was one of several religious institutions where carnal men had perverted God's plan of giving into a religious Pyramid Scheme. After a while, the hype became their truth as deception ruled over hearts and minds. Now, that hype was being threatened. Loyalty and obedience had to be rekindled at all cost.

The First Lady had been trying for weeks to convince her husband that he should meet with the ministry board regarding the issue. Finally, at a loss for what to do, Pastor Riche accepted the counsel of his wife.

It was agreed that the church leaders would be summoned to the Riche home to strategize. Mrs. Riche couldn't wait to call the caterers and dispatch invitations. She had a plan.

Lorraine Riche knew how to throw a bash. On the evening of their gathering, the church leaders and their wives were seated around an elaborately appointed dinner table. Mrs. Riche had informed her husband that their daughters, Jewell, 24, and Cookie, 26, would join the party. Daddy Riche, who adored his girls, could not have been more delighted.

When sufficient praise had gone up for the prime rib and lobster, it was time to get down to business. Gordon Riche was somber and foreboding as he addressed the group.

"Well, my friends, you all know the problem that we are facing regarding our decreasing funds. It's going to take some bold action to keep us from going under. After some consideration, I've come to the conclusion that Kingdom Glory Temple needs to start an outreach program, but not in the traditional sense."

Pastor Riche was well aware that none of them were interested in actually reaching out to those in need. So he proceeded to qualify his opening statement.

"My friends, what we need is an in-house outreach. We've got to somehow reach out beyond the front rows of our assembly to reassure the lay congregants that we can relate to them, and that we are operating in the will of God for their lives.

Just consider the lessons of the recent elections. If our membership begins to lose faith in our trickle down principle for giving, our funding base will be undermined and possibly destroyed. They must never come to doubt the leadership of God's anointed and his associates."

The pastor then pointed around the table for emphasis. As the board members nodded their agreement, he continued.

"The people must be reminded that they will never be blessed if they stop being a blessing. We must keep this vision of steadfast faithful giving deeply planted in their hearts and minds!"

Pastor Riche then acknowledged the raised hand of Deacon Miller, who timidly cleared his throat before speaking. "Well, Pastor Riche, the time is almost here for the annual *Vision for Giving*, four-part seminar."

"Deacon Miller, our intake is at a record low. When I finally take my seat each week, the baskets are not as heavy with cash and your arms are not as heavy with bodies as they used to be. We need to do more than the seminar this year."

The other board members shuffled in their seats and stared around the room.

"Honey, may I speak?" The soft voice of First lady Lorraine relieved the uncomfortable silence.

"Of course, my dear, I value your input." He smiled across the table at his wife of 30 years.

"Well, I think we need to engage individuals from the very group we are trying to affect."

Pastor Riche did not understand at first, but he motioned for her to continue.

"Well, we have intercessors that could be used to pray. We've all heard testimonies of their effectiveness. There's obviously something to it."

Minister Charles immediately raised his hand and received clearance to speak.

"Uh, respectfully, First Lady, we are not talking about some little prayer requests. Rather, what we need here is comprehensive strategy for church direction. These praying women are neither licensed nor ordained. How can they help?"

But, Pastor Riche was beginning to get it.

"Hold up, Minister Charles, I think my wife may be on to something here. If the folks see and hear other people like themselves praying for our *Vision for Giving*, that could be a good thing. Besides, does anyone else have a better idea?"

No one else had any ideas.

"Please, go on, my dear."

For a second, the handsome couple drank each other in. Eyes locked in mutual affection caused them to almost forget their guests.

"Thank you, Gordon. I do have something more to share."

Lorraine Riche smiled around the table and continued.

"I believe that we have been neglecting a hidden treasure in our midst. Our two daughters, Jewell and Cookie, are among our most overlooked assets. I think we should use them toward this effort.

After all, they are both college-educated with high profile jobs where they are paid to influence people on a regular basis. Why not use their ability to influence others for the kingdom?"

She paused only briefly for emphasis.

"Here's my plan. Our official membership is 75 percent female. Why don't we have the girls meet with these intercessors to start a Women's Prayer Fellowship?

Cookie and Jewell could instill the *Vision for Giving* into these women using a sort of mentor-to-mentee impartation approach. Then, the intercessors could be used to pray for the vision before the congregation each week."

Lorraine paused briefly to allow for comments. When none came forth, she continued.

"Furthermore, I believe these women would be blessed by their mere interaction with our girls. Once the group is up and running, who knows where it could lead? Cookie and Jewell are poised to make their mark on corporate America. They are model examples for those women in the back pews, who need to pull themselves up by their own bootstraps!

Listen, gentlemen, you've laid hands; you've preached and taught until you're blue in the face. The offerings are still going down. Why not try marketing the message using strategic prayer?"

Then, gushing with pride at Jewell and Cookie, she continued. "Furthermore, our girls are living holy and chaste. This fact alone has surely earned them the right to lead."

First Lady Lorraine then lowered her head in a display of modesty.

The *holy and chaste* comment did not go over too well with some of the other wives whose daughters were running buck wild.

But, the general consensus was that Jewell and Cookie Riche were the last two adult virgins left at Kingdom Glory Temple. So, the other women kept silent as the First Lady concluded.

"I took the liberty of asking Jewell and Cookie if they'd be willing to give of their time, and they agreed, – providing you all agree of course."

Jewell and Cookie then nodded, smiling their lovely smiles at the dinner guests.

An audible sigh of relief drifted round the table. It was unanimously decided that the Riche sisters would head up the formation of the Kingdom Glory Temple Women's Prayer Fellowship. The board members could not believe their good fortune. A plan of action had been agreed upon and they weren't tasked to do anything.

Now they were able to really enjoy their evening. And so, as crystal goblets tapped ever so lightly, and sterling flatware met fine china, they finished their meal in relaxed satisfaction.

Although the Riche girls earned enough money to live on their own, they preferred the residence provided by their parents, via Kingdom Glory Temple.

All things considered, they made a fine pair of whitewashed cups. Their virginal status had nothing to do with consecration to God. No, they were holding out for successful, preferably church-going husbands, willing and able to keep them in the luxury they were accustomed to. The sisters vowed to either date in those circles or not at all. As a result, they rarely dated.

The sisters were drop dead gorgeous and cold as ice. But, they could conjure up a fiery performance on cue. All it took was the right prompt from the key board and they were cutting a furious rug in their Jimmy Choo pumps.

When Daddy Riche cried out from the pulpit, no one could hit the floor or speak in an unknown tongue like Jewell and Cookie. And, after it was over, every hair fell fall back into place as they were raised to their seats without a wrinkle.

Lorraine Riche sang lead in the choir, most Sundays. Prior to becoming First Lady, she'd made a name for herself, singing backup for several R&B recording artists. And Lorraine could still blow.

But, despite their impressive assets, and undaunted self-love, the Riches were on a shaky descent from the pedestal as their grip on the adult congregants continued to weaken. The Woman's Prayer Fellowship would have its work cut out.

Only the most gullible young ladies saw Jewell and Cookie as role models, worthy of leading a ministry. These kids saw the sisters as glamorous church divas who they hoped to rub shoulders with. It never occurred to them that they were of no importance to their self-absorbed idols.

In the weeks leading up to the first planning meeting, Pastor Riche briefed his daughters carefully. The intercessors would need to be primed for the impartation of the vision so that that it became life to them. The girls promised to deliver.

The sisters were all keyed up before the kick-off. After several dress rehearsals, they'd finally decided what to wear. Then they addressed the other issues.

Cookie drafted a PowerPoint presentation consisting of a fifteen minute marketing tutorial reworked from her office files. Each slide talked about team work, loyalty, and how the individual should advance the vision of leadership for the good of the whole.

She had added the appropriate religious verbiage including the *Touch not my anointed*, warning. That exhortation, taken out of context, was widely used to keep abused sheep under submission.

Jewell had created a ministry color scheme and some potential logos to run by her sister. She entered Cookie's bedroom suite and plopped down on the king-sized bed, watching her sister brush her hair.

"What's up with you, big sister? All day you've been muttering some foolishness about the word, *love*."

Cookie put down her brush and turned around to face her baby sister.

"Well, Jewell, last night after I'd finished the slide presentation, I started getting bored. So, I began writing down words and playing with their letters to come up with new meanings.

Check this out, I came up with a new acronym for the word, *love*. Would you like to hear it?"

"Why, yes, of course I would."

"Okay, hear it goes. L.O.V.E. equals *Liberal Offerings to the Victimized Echelons!*"

Jewell's pretty jaw dropped in shock for a split second, and then she let out a howl. "Oh, Cookie, that is brilliant girl. I felt that way down in my soul."

"I know girl, I amaze myself sometimes!"

That comment brought on more laughter as Jewell motioned for her sister to join her on the bed. Poking fun at the have-nots always brought them closer together. They were still for a moment, smiling up at the over-sized crystal chandelier.

"Hey, Jewell, remember Daddy's teaching series called *Sloppy-Agape?*"

"Of course, my favorite part was the sermon called "Ray-Ray and Shameka – Exposed.""

"Oh, girl…!"

With that, the two giggled all over Cookie's silk duvet, pleased as punch with themselves and very sure of their tomorrow.

Three intercessors had been handpicked by the First Lady (or so it appeared) to serve on the ministry start-up committee. She knew nothing about them except that they had received the most positive testimony from people they'd prayed for.

In actuality, Lena Fulton was a single mother with two and a half jobs. Lena was hungry for the word and destined to teach it.

Florence Miller was a middle aged, empty-nest wife whose wings had been clipped years ago by an unsaved husband. God had called her to be a mother of the church.

Then there was Lois Campbell, whom God had relocated from the Big Apple. Lois loved God much for she'd been forgiven much.

Because Lena's half job ended at 12:00 noon on Saturday, the meeting was set for 1:30 pm. None of the three women drove or had access to a car. By the time they reached Kingdom Glory Temple by bus, the Riche girls were all set up with their PowerPoint slides and color swatches.

Cookie was the first to stand up before the trio of women. "Hello, ladies, thank you so much for coming to this kick-off planning meeting. I hope that we will get a lot accomplished today as far as laying down a foundation for our fellowship. So let's get to work!" As she reached for her material, Florence asked if they could open with a prayer.

"Why, of course, would you please do the honors?"

Oh darn, thought Jewell. *Cookie has forgotten that we were supposed to open in prayer.* Pastor Riche had given them the words to pray.

Florence began. "Dear Lord, first we want to praise you right now, for who you are. Thank you for seeing us safely here. We know that where two or more are gathered in your name, you will be in the midst. And so we ask that you lead us and guide us into all truth. Bring understanding to our hearts and give us ears to hear as you instruct us about what will please you.

Some of us are feeling a little weary and heavy laden, but you told us that we can come to you for rest. Oh God, let us not end this day the way we started. In Jesus' name, we humbly pray."

Lois and Lena offered a heartfelt "Amen." Cookie and Jewell, who hated long prayers, uttered a sigh of relief.

The PowerPoint tutorial was presented next. Cookie's slides went over like a lead balloon. The intercessors offered no questions or comments.

Well, maybe that's a good thing. Ultimately, they don't have to understand why they do what they do, as long as they do it. Cookie took her seat, reassured by that thought.

Then, Jewell came forth, handing out the color swatches of purple, gold, and red.

"I chose these colors to represent the principles of our church: Royalty, Riches, and the Blood, of course, – not to mention a little Pucci vibe."

Jewell winked at Cookie, who chuckled at her sister's wit. Of course their private joke was never intended for the intercessors who probably bought their clothes at Wal-Mart, and had never heard of Emilio Pucci.

Cookie was up again to present the two logo slides.

"Jewell came up with a couple of possible logos to capture what our fellowship would eventually be about. We hope to one day be a full-fledged women's ministry. So, here we go."

One slide depicted a lovely maiden on a balcony lowering her golden cross chain belt down to a throng of pleading women. The other slide depicted a well-toned female in designer athletic wear beckoning a crowd of less shapely women to follow her on to the Kingdom Glory Track.

Again, there was no response. Cookie and Jewell were beginning to wonder if they were casting their pearls before swine. The three women of God stared back and forth from the slides to the facilitators until Cookie broke the silence.

"Well, we don't have to decide on any of this right now."

Florence then asked a question. "Sister Cookie, can you tell us more about the purpose of this group?"

"Well, Sister Florence, like the Pastor announced, this is the kick-off planning meeting to launch the Kingdom Glory Temple Women's Prayer Fellowship."

"Yes, Sister Cookie, but what are we hoping to accomplish in this fellowship?"

"Well, initially we are going to learn to pray for the vision of our anointed leadership to prevail in the church. If the leadership is threatened, the church can't prevail."

"What vision would that be, Sister Cookie?"

"Well, the *Vision for Giving,* of course! Ladies, we need for things to continue as they have been without any discord, especially regarding our faithful dedication to giving."

Lena then spoke up. "What about change?"

"Sister Lena, I'm not quite sure what you mean by change. Why would things need to change?"

"Well, Sister Cookie, things may need to change when what we've been doing is not working."

Pursing her lips at the audacity of Lena's comment, Cookie calmed herself and considered how she should respond. She decided to have Lena elaborate.

"Sister Lena, can you please be more specific? Maybe give us an example?"

"Well, for instance, at Kingdom Glory Temple we're taught that we must care for the needs of the church before we care for our family's needs. But the needs of the church seem more like wants that never cease.

As a result some families are suffering, but they're told that their suffering is due to a lack of faith. So they don't get any help from our church. Then they're criticized harshly for going to another ministry for help or for even visiting another church."

At that point, Jewell got up to stand with her sister. In an attempt to control her self-righteous indignation, she began to patronize.

"We should take care not to concern ourselves with things that do not concern us. There is an order in the church where we look to the leaders to stand in the gap for us, for our own good. There is a reason why God places leaders over His people.

They alone are anointed to decide what is best for us. That includes whether change is needed or not. Their wisdom should never be questioned. I believe this concept was fully explained in the teaching slides."

"But, Sister Jewell, isn't it the job of the Holy Spirit to lead us into all truth?"

"Sister Lena, the ministers are led by the Spirit in all these things."

"But, Sister Jewell wasn't the Spirit given to lead each of us? Doesn't the royal priesthood include everyone? Just last night I was reading about the Bereans, what about them?"

Jewell looked over at Cookie, who was also clueless. "The Bereans – who or what are the Bereans?"

"Well, Sister Jewell, the Bible said the Bereans were of more noble character because they received the message eagerly and examined the Scriptures every day to see if what Paul said was true. It's there in Acts 17:11."

Feeling a bit agitated, and in over their heads, the two huddled together for a few seconds, and then Cookie made an announcement.

"I feel it's time to bring our first meeting to a close."

But, she could not afford to deviate from Pastor Riche's instructions again. It had been the job of the Riche daughters to gain any information on the three women that might be relevant to their preparation as intercessors for the vision. That information would be useful as the women were prayed over.

"Now, before you leave, God has a word for each of you that will help to equip you for your important role. Just this morning our pastor prayed and anointed Jewell and me so that we might impart something specific to each of you. This is a Rhema word and should not be taken lightly.

As we are taught over and over, only those who receive will be blessed. So let's stand and expect the Spirit to fall!"

Pastor Riche liked to preface his altar calls with that exhortation. And everyone got the message – hit the floor by faith even if you don't feel it.

Jewel then grabbed a gilded vile of EVOO. Not used to the process, she soaked her and Cookie's hands. Trying not to get oil on their designer outfits, they gingerly approached God's women, who were about to take their last bow before a fake anointing.

First, Jewel laid hands on Lena who went limp by rote. Nevertheless, it gave Jewell a power rush, and she began to speak as the flesh gave her utterance.

"I come against the spirit of illegitimacy, any fornication remnant, the spirit of lack and most of all, confusion over the word. Please make a way in Lena's work schedule for her to attend Bible study so that she can gain a better understanding as she sits at the pastor's feet, Amen."

Next Cookie laid hands on Florence, who obediently collapsed as much as her swollen knees would allow. Then Cookie went in for the kill.

"Please have mercy on this woman who is unequally yoked to an unsaved man. Please release the tithe from his wallet so that the curse can be lifted from her as well as their children and grandchildren. Until then Kingdom Glory Temple will not despise her widow's mite offerings, Amen."

Wow, this is good stuff, thought the pair. After a rigorous dance around Lena and Florence, they'd begun to sweat through their silk camisoles and were feeling pretty bold.

Turning away from the first two women, they approached Lois. Lois was standing there with eyes closed and hands lifted in total praise. Just as they raised their acrylic tipped claws to strike, an unspoken word pierced the atmosphere and routed the enemy.

This one is already slain and will not abide your touch. They stopped in their tracks and backed off.

And so, that concluded the kick-off meeting of the Kingdom Glory Temple Women's Prayer Fellowship.

However, the prayers of the faithful were not in vain. None of God's servants would end that day the way they started it!

Lena went home with a fierce determination to seek the Spirit regarding Scripture and its application. She would study to show herself approved and encourage others to do the same.

Florence left Kingdom Glory Temple inconsolable regarding her so-called curse. But Jesus would set things straight in her prayer closet that evening and she'd be changed forever.

And last, but not least, Lois went to her bed thanking God for His confirmation and direction regarding her first kingdom assignment.

Jewel and Cookie watched from the church lobby as the three intercessors boarded the crowded MARTA bus.

"Thank goodness, no one asked for a ride. God only knows where they live."

"I know that's right."

"You know Cookie, Daddy will have to deal with Lena's obsession over Scripture references."

"Yes, she was starting to confuse me. I mean I'm an M.B.A, not a theologian."

"I heard that; my field is Fashion Merchandising. Lena just needs to trust the women who are clearly walking in victory and use us as examples for her own life.

Hello! I mean, she's a *knock off* nightmare with a pew full of Bebe's kids!"

"You are so bad, little sister – but so right!"

Then, Cookie gave a little pout, twisting her auburn curls. "I almost felt sorry for Florence, suffering under a husband that won't tithe."

"I know, girl! Even if he's not saved and doesn't come to church, he should send the tenth. Why that's just Biblical, right?"

Suddenly, Jewell's pretty face was burdened.

"Cookie, what do you think of Lois, that quiet one? She gives me the creeps."

"Yep, that one may be trouble. I don't even know what kind of spirit I sensed there."

"I'd say it's a spirit of one who does not know her place. There's usually one in every group."

It was a lovely afternoon. The two sisters walked out to their reserved parking areas. Both were wondering if they should tell their father about Lois. But, what was there to tell – that something prevented them from touching her?

"Jewell, it may take a minute before these women can be called upon to pray for the vision. After all, this was just the first meeting.

Let's tell Daddy that we are very committed to the cause and confident that the will of God will soon prevail."

"That sounds good to me, big sister."

Suddenly, Cookie got a brainstorm. "You know, after all that spiritual warfare I need a pick-me-up."

"What do you have in mind, Cookie? You know the malls are packed on Saturdays."

"Oh, stop, Jewell!"

"Well, what then?"

Cookie tossed her high-end weave over one eye and smiled mischievously. "Starbuck's anyone? They have a new blend out today!"

"Well, let's go then. And Cooke, all things considered I think we made a great team today."

"I think so, too, baby sister. Oh, come here and give us a hug."

Feeling super blessed and satisfied, the sisters kissed cheeks and patted backs, their gold charm bracelets clanging in the air.

And, then, the pretty occupants of *Beamers Three and Four for the Kingdom* set out toward Peachtree Street to fill their empty cups.

The end…TBD

APPENDEX
Suggested Questions for Reading Groups

Crossroads

1. Jim Crow continued the breakdown of the black family after slavery ended.
    - What drove Mamie to keep her rape from Nate – fear or love?
    - Was Nate an Uncle Tom for not avenging his wife's rape?
    - How successful were they as parents?
2. Isaac and Dana dealt with a more subtle form of racism in the North.
    - What were they able to "bring to the table" in marriage to benefit their Southern born spouses?
3. How valid is Kitty's assessment of the Christian view of interracial marriage?
4. Luke compares his lost years to a "Trojan horse without a cause."
    - What did he mean?
5. Dana hears Luke's story in 3rd person narrative. Mamie has no dialog.
    - How does the narrative transform his individual story into a broader ethnic epitaph?
    - What is the significance of Mamie's silence?
6. Luke had acquired the love of Dana, Isaac, and Kitty before they knew he was black.
    - Why is that significant?
    - What kept Luke from rejecting his blackness, even as he passed for white?
    - Does skin color variance still affect relationships within the black community?
7. Kitty and Luke descended from two families confronted with the same evil.
    - How did one family resist and the other succumb?
    - Which family did which?
8. Isaac told Luke that he had chosen a different pulpit from his father.

- Why did the Civil Rights Movement use different pulpits or platforms to accomplish its goals?
9. Luke and Dana Prince were especially vulnerable, as they made their way to Mississippi in the summer of 1963.
    - What would make them a greater target than Isaac and Kitty?
    - Discuss the importance of that kick in Dana's womb.

Sifting the Squeeze
1. Tobias Yearwood abandoned his family and never looked back.
    - How did this rejection shape Wilson and Tina as adults?
    - What did Wilson fear most, and why?
    - How did Wilson's dependence on "self" feed his depravity?
2. Tyra was easy prey to Wilson's advances.
    - What internal and external factors caused her to fall under his spell?
    - How did these factors influence her attitude after she became sexually involved with Wilson?
3. Sowing and reaping is a prevalent thread throughout the story.
    - How is this principle manipulated by Wilson, Tyra, and Pastor Bush?
4. Abby's first intervention with Tyra falls short, but she later plays a significant role in her cousin's deliverance.
    - How did her next intervention differ?
    - How did Tyra's fast differ from Abby's?
5. How did the tears shed by Tyra at Living Word, differ from the tears she shed at the House of Grace?
6. How significant is the timing of Wilson's ring purchase?
7. What might the removal of Wilson's façade towards the end of the story suggest?
8. What does it mean to be sifted in the Biblical sense?

Not by Works
1. From Nola and Jean's perspective, how important was faith in Christ to those who experienced the turbulent events of

the 1960s?

2. How valuable is Jean's insight as she responds to Nola's confession regarding her gift of singleness?

3. What correlation does the story make between worship, knowing God's will, and being fruitful?

4. How does Nola's lifestyle shatter the stereotypical images of women who are living chaste and consecrated to God?

5. Nola and Seth's marriage is described as being *divinely orchestrated*.
   - What characteristics do Nola and Seth demonstrate that confirm their readiness for marriage?
   - How can you see their individual gifts being strengthened in marriage?

6. What does the story reveal about the importance of seasons and preparation in the lives of God's people?

Offerings

1. Gabi and Faith grew up in the same household.
   - What do their opposite lifestyles say about the election of God?

2. Faith made a decision to call herself Effie.
   - Why do you think she decided to name herself?
   - How did it speak to her confused sense of identity?

3. Faith blamed others for her situation in life.
   - How was her inability to be held accountable a self-destructive force in her life?

4. Ramona and Rory suffered as a result of Faith's issues. Consider the altar scene at Rory's dedication.
   - How widespread is this form of parental deficiency?
   - Why is it so important to have intercessors standing in the gap?

5. The story bears witness to God's love and grace.
   - What evidence of God's willingness to forgive sin did Faith refuse to acknowledge?
   - How did Faith's belief that she was owed something prevent her from accepting Jesus and His gift of salvation?

6. The enemy dwells in secrecy, holding captives hostage to the fear of exposure.
   - How did Gabi's obedient testimony disarm the powers of darkness and glorify God?

7. When Faith appeared at the car, was there more that Gabi could or should have done?
8. Right before Lois ran to the altar, we saw the first evidence of an inner struggle between Faith and Effie. This struggle continues in the final scene of the story
   • What might this suggest for Faith and her children?

Gongs and Cymbals

1. How is Scripture twisted by Pastor Riche and his staff to abuse their position of leadership and promote their own agenda?
2. In James 3:1 the Bible offers a warning regarding teachers.
   • Why do you think teachers will be judged more harshly?
   • Do you think Pastor Riche's *Vision for Giving* agrees with Biblical principles?
3. What correlation can be made between the trickle-down theory in politics, and how it is at work at Kingdom Glory Temple?
4. What does the attitude toward prayer, held by the leaders of KGT reveal about them?
5. It became obvious that Pastor Riche was losing control over the members of KGT.
   • What signs of unrest were present?
   • What did the First Lady's plan to regain control suggest about her relationship to God?
6. What was the irony of Lorraine Riche's comment about the need for the women in her church to pull themselves up by their own bootstraps?
7. How do the Riche women exemplify the principle of false virtue appearing real?
8. How does Cookie's LOVE acronym mock the true meaning of God's love and His concern for those who are in need?
9. The three intercessors were handpicked for the Women's Fellowship Group.
   • Who really handpicked them?
   • What might that suggest regarding the future of KGT?

Vertical Hold

1. How is the keeping power of God and His allowance for repentance demonstrated in each of the five stories?

2. What correlation do you see between tribulation and preparation for ministry demonstrated throughout the book?

3. Consider the characters in these stories and then complete the sentences below:
   - I can identify most of all with _____ because_____.
   - I can identify least of all with_____ because_____.

4. Consider the characters you selected above.
   - How do you envision the development of these characters as their lives continue beyond the pages of *Vertical Hold?*

Made in the USA
Lexington, KY
20 June 2017